This book should be returned to any branch of the
Lancashire County Library on or before the date

13 ~~~ 2017		Ske
1 NOV 17		11/15

Lancashire County Library
Bowran Street
Preston PR1 2UX
www.lancashire.gov.uk/libraries

"Morning, Sleeping Beauty." Slade gave a lopsided, almost self-deriding grin. "Some night, eh?"

Taylor groaned and pulled a pillow over her head, then just peered out from behind it. "Tell me that wasn't real."

He shrugged his magnificent shoulders. "That wasn't real…"

Dropping the pillow, but hanging on tightly to the sheet, she let out a surprised sigh of relief.

"But if by 'that' you're referring to our wedding at the North Pole Christmas Bliss Wedding Chapel…" The words came out with a mixture of amusement and shock, as if he couldn't quite believe what they'd done either. "Well, according to our marriage certificate, that was *very* real."

Keeping the covers tucked securely around her, Taylor sat up. A wave of nausea smacked her insides. He stood there, looking sexy as sin, and she was going to throw up.

Great. Just flipping great.

Dear Reader,

We've all heard that old saying: 'What happens in Vegas, stays in Vegas.' But it doesn't always... Sometimes a girl marries the wrong man who might *just* end up being the right man!

Slade Sain is about as opposite to what Taylor Anderson wants in a man as he can possibly be. Except that he's sexy as sin, makes her feel good about herself, and he's a fantastic, compassionate oncologist. Now he's her husband. So this year all she wants for Christmas is a quickie divorce and for what happened in Vegas truly to stay in Vegas.

Slade dedicated his life to breast cancer research at the tender age of twelve, when his mother died from the horrible disease. He knows the path his life is destined to take. Getting married is a bump on that road he never intended to travel over. Sure, Taylor has always fascinated him—but he's a good-time guy, not a for ever kind of man. She's vulnerable, a single mum, and still believes in Christmas. He should have known better. Only maybe his heart has been headed in the right direction all along...

I hope you enjoy their story, and that Santa stuffs your stockings with all the things you really want.

Merry Christmas!

Janice

WINTER WEDDING IN VEGAS

BY
JANICE LYNN

First published in Great Britain 2015
by Mills & Boon, an imprint of Harlequin (UK) Limited,
Eton House, 18-24 Paradise Road, Richmond, Surrey, TW9 1SR

© 2015 Janice Lynn

ISBN: 978-0-263-25922-3

Harlequin (UK) Limited's policy is to use papers that are natural,
renewable and recyclable products and made from wood grown in
sustainable forests. The logging and manufacturing processes conform
to the legal environmental regulations of the country of origin.

Printed and bound in Great Britain
by CPI Antony Rowe, Chippenham, Wiltshire

Janice Lynn has a Masters in Nursing from Vanderbilt University, and works as a nurse practitioner in a family practice. She lives in the southern United States with her husband, their four children, their Jack Russell—appropriately named Trouble—and a lot of unnamed dust bunnies that have moved in since she started her writing career. To find out more about Janice and her writing visit janicelynn.com.

Books by Janice Lynn

Mills & Boon Medical Romance

Dr Di Angelo's Baby Bombshell
Officer, Gentleman...Surgeon!
The Nurse Who Saved Christmas
Doctor's Damsel in Distress
Flirting with the Society Doctor
Challenging the Nurse's Rules
NYC Angels: The Heiress's Baby Scandal
The ER's Newest Dad
Flirting with the Doc of Her Dreams
New York Doc to Blushing Bride

Visit the Author Profile page at millsandboon.co.uk for more titles.

Janice won The National Readers' Choice Award for her first book
The Doctor's Pregnancy Bombshell

To my favourite nurse, Joni Sain!
You rock!!!

**Praise for
Janice Lynn**

'Fun, witty and sexy… A heartfelt, sensual and
compelling read.'
—*GoodReads* on
NYC Angels: The Heiress's Baby Scandal

'A sweet and beautiful romance that will steal your heart.'
—*HarlequinJunkie* on
NYC Angels: The Heiress's Baby Scandal

CHAPTER ONE

Dr. Taylor Anderson woke from the craziest dream she'd ever had. Apparently sleeping in a glitzy Las Vegas hotel stretched one's inner imagination beyond all reason.

Married. Her. To Dr. Slade Sain.

As if.

The man was such a player, she wouldn't date him, much less consider a more serious relationship with the likes of him. Sure, he was gorgeous, invaded her deepest, darkest dreams from time to time, but the man's little black book had more phone numbers than the Yellow Pages.

If and when she married, no way would she make the same relationship mistakes she had made during medical school. Never again was she walking down that painful path of inevitable unfaithfulness from a man she should have known better than to trust.

Yet her mind warned that last night hadn't been a dream, that she had married Slade.

Last night she'd drowned her awkwardness around him. She rarely drank, but she'd felt so self-conscious surrounded by Slade and her colleagues in a social setting, that she had overimbibed. She didn't think she'd been out and out drunk, but she hadn't been herself.

These days, the real her was quiet and reserved, steady and stable. Responsible. Not the kind of woman to go to a tacky Sin City year-round Christmas-themed wedding chapel and marry a man she respected as a brilliant oncologist, had found unbelievably attractive from the moment she'd first laid eyes on him, but thought as cheesy as the Jolly Old Saint Nick who'd, apparently, also been an ordained minister. Who knew?

Mentally, she counted to ten, took a deep breath, and opened her eyes. She was in her hotel room queen-size bed and Sexy Slade Sain was nowhere in sight.

She glanced at the opposite side of the bed. The covers were so tangled, who knew if there had been anyone other than herself beneath the sheets? Just because she usually woke with the bedcovers almost as neat as when she'd crawled between them didn't mean a thing. Really.

She wasn't in denial. No way.

Neither did the fact she was in the middle of the bed, sort of diagonally, and sprawled out. Naked. What had she done with her clothes?

What had she done with her naked body?

A knock sounded on the door leading out of the room. Feeling like she was suffering a mini–heart attack, Taylor grabbed at the tangled sheets.

"Room service," a male voice called through the door.

Room service? She pulled the covers tightly around her body. She hadn't ordered room service.

The bathroom door opened and a damp, dark-haired pin-up calendar model wearing only a towel—dear sweet heaven, the man had a fine set of shoulders and six-pack!—undid the safety chain.

Slade was in her hotel room. Naked beneath the towel and he was buff. The towel riding low around his waist, covering his perfect butt, his perfect… She gulped back saliva pooling in her mouth.

Despite her desperate clinging to denial of the cold hard facts she'd been willfully repressing, she knew exactly what she'd done with her naked body. What she'd done with *his* naked body. Why her bedsheets were so tangled. The details of how she'd come to the conclusion that marrying Slade was a logical decision might be a little fuzzy, but she'd known exactly what she'd been doing when Slade's mouth had taken hers. Hot, sweaty, blow-your-mind sex, that's what she'd done. With Slade. As much as her brain was screaming *No!* her body shouted, *Encore!*

"That was quick," Mr. Multiple Orgasms praised the hotel employee pushing a cart into the room. He stopped the man just inside the doorway. "I'll take it from here."

The pressure in Taylor's head throbbed to where at any moment she was going to form and rupture an aneurysm. Slade's wife. This had to be a nightmare. Or a joke. Or a mistake they could rectify with an annulment.

Could a couple get an annulment if they'd spent the night in bed, performing exotic yoga moves with energetic bursts of pleasurable cardio?

She closed her eyes and let images from the night before wash over her, of Slade unlocking her hotel room door, sweeping her off her feet, and carrying her to the bed and stripping off her clothes. She'd giggled and kissed his neck when he'd carried her across the threshold. Then he'd kissed her. Really, deeply kissed her. Even now she could recall the feel of his lips against hers, the feel of his body against hers, his spicy male scent. Heat rose, flushing her face, ears and much more feminine parts.

They so wouldn't qualify for an annulment.

Wow at the moves the man had hidden inside that fabulous body. His hands were magic. Pure magic. His mouth? Magic. Just *wow*.

She cracked open an eyelid to steal a peek. He tipped the man from Room Service from his wallet on the dresser, closed the door, turned and caught her staring.

"Morning, Sleeping Beauty." He gave a lopsided, almost self-deriding grin. "Some night, eh?"

She groaned and pulled a pillow over her head to where she just peered out from behind it. "Tell me that wasn't real."

He shrugged his magnificent shoulders. "That wasn't real."

Dropping the pillow but hanging on tightly to the sheet, she let out a surprised sigh of relief.

"But if by 'that' you're referring to our wedding at the North Pole Christmas Bliss Wedding Chapel—" the words came out with a mixture of amusement and shock, as if he couldn't quite believe what they'd done either "—well, according to our marriage certificate, that was very real."

Keeping the covers tucked securely around her, Taylor sat up. A wave of nausea smacked her insides. He stood there looking sexy as sin and she was going to barf. Great. Just flipping great.

"One minute we were kissing in the limo surrounded by Christmas music and that crazy peppermint spray the driver kept showering us with, the next we're getting married so we could have sex. Great sex, by the way. You blew me away." His blue eyes sparkling with mischievous intent, he moved toward her and she shook her head in horrified denial.

"Get back," she warned, covers clutched to her chest with one hand and the other outstretched as if warding off an evil spirit. Sure, there was a part of her that was thrilled that he'd enjoyed their night as much as she had, but it was morning. The morning after. And they'd gotten married. "That's crazy. We didn't have to get married to have sex."

Pausing, he scratched his head as if confused. "Not that I don't agree with you, but that's not what you said last night in the limo."

The movement of his arm flexed muscles along his chest and abdomen and sent a wave of tingles through her body, but that wasn't why she gulped again. She was just…thirsty? Parched. Still fighting the urge to barf. Forcing her eyes to focus on his face and not the rest of him, she blinked. The flicker of awareness in his blue eyes warned he knew exactly what she had been looking at, what she'd been thinking, and he wasn't immune to her thoughts.

"You told me you wouldn't have sex with me unless we were married," he reminded her.

She had said that. In the midst of his hot, lust-provoking kisses she'd thrown down her gauntlet, expecting him to run or laugh in her face. "So you married me?"

He glanced down at the cheap band on his left hand and shrugged. "Obviously."

Not that he sounded any happier about it than she felt, but someone should shoot her now. She was wearing a ring, too. A simple golden band on the wedding finger of her left hand. Because she was married. To Slade.

Slade was not the man of her dreams, was not someone she'd carefully chosen to spend the rest of her life based upon well-thought-out criteria. He was exactly what she avoided even dating because men like Slade didn't jibe with her life plans. How could she have had such a huge lapse of judgement?

The metal hugging her finger tightened to painful proportions. At any moment her finger was going to turn blue and drop off from lack of blood flow. Seriously.

She went to remove the ring, but couldn't bring herself to do it. Why, she couldn't exactly say. Probably the same insanity that had had her saying "I do" to a man she should have been screaming "I don't" at. Besides, she'd probably have to buy a stick of butter before the thing would budge.

"We should talk about this." He glanced at his watch. "But we have our presentation in just over an hour. You should eat."

She glanced at the bedside table's digital clock. Crap. She'd slept much later than normal. Then again, she'd stayed up much later than normal.

Nothing had been normal about the night before. It had been as if she'd been watching someone else do all the things she'd done, as if it had all been a fantasy, not real.

"You have to go to your room," she told him, needing to be away from his watchful blue gaze.

"I'm in my room." He shifted his weight and her attention dropped to where the towel was tucked in at his waist. His amazing, narrow waist that sported abs no doctor should boast. Abs like those belonged on sport stars and models, not white-collar professionals who saw cancer patients all day. "Last night we arranged for the hotel staff to move my things into your room while we're in class today."

They had stopped by the front desk and requested that. Wincing, her gaze shot to his.

"No." She was going to throw up. Really she was. How was she going to explain this to Gracie? She grimaced. "I don't want you in my room."

"Understood." He looked as if he really didn't want to be there either. "But we're married."

"Married" had come out sounding much like a dirty word, like someone who'd just been given a deadly diagnosis.

Guilt hit Taylor. She had told him she wouldn't have sex with him unless they were married. But wasn't marriage a bit far for a man to go just to get laid? He had a busy revolving door to his bedroom so he couldn't have been that desperate for sex. He must have been as inebriated as she had.

"How did we end up married?" she asked, pulling the bedcovers up to her neck. The less he could see of her the better. She already felt exposed.

"You told me you wanted to have sex with me, but that you wouldn't unless we were married. Our elfish limo driver said he knew a place that could take care of a last-minute license and we happened to be right outside it. We got married and had sex. You know this. You were there."

If she'd been into one-night stands, last night would have been amazing. But she wasn't. She was a mature, professional doctor who had learned her life lessons the hard way and had a beautiful little girl she was raising by herself to prove it. She'd vowed she wouldn't have sex again without being married first. Had she foolishly believed marriage would protect her from future heartbreak?

She'd wanted Slade so much. Had possibly wanted him for months, although she'd never admitted as much to herself. When their pointy-eared three-and-a-half-foot-tall limo driver had taken them to the chapel, she'd looked at Slade, expecting him to laugh at her condition.

When she'd seen him actually seriously considering marrying her just to have sex with her, a big chunk of the protective ice she'd frozen around her heart had melted, leaving her vulnerable and wanting what she'd seen in his eyes. Whether it had been the alcohol, the Christmas magic everywhere, or just Vegas madness, she'd wanted to marry Slade the night before. It made no logical sense, but she'd wanted him to want her enough to walk down the aisle to have her.

"We were drunk," she offered as an out. "We can get an annulment because we were drunk."

His expression pained, he narrowed his gaze. "Maybe."

His hands went to his hips and, again, she had to force her eyes upward to keep them from wandering lower than his face. The man was beautiful, she'd give him that.

"I wasn't sober," she persisted, clinging to the fact that she hadn't been in her right mind. She wasn't in her right mind now either. Her head hurt and, crazy as it was, she wanted him, but she couldn't tell him that. "Regardless, I want a divorce."

Raking his fingers through his towel-dried hair, Slade eyed Taylor grasping the covers to her beautiful body as if she expected him to rip them off and demand she succumb to his marital rights whether she wanted him or not. Did she really think so poorly of him? Despite the fact he'd not been able to say "I do" fast enough the night before, he didn't want to be married any more than she apparently did.

Probably less.

Sure, he'd been attracted from the moment he'd met her.

But although he'd have sworn she felt a similar spark, she'd brushed off his attempts to further their relationship.

Until last night.

Last night she'd looked at him and he'd felt captivated, needy, as if under a spell he hadn't been able to snap out of.

He took a deep breath. "A divorce works for me. A wife is not something I planned to bring back from Vegas."

Or from anywhere. He had his future mapped out and a wife didn't fit anywhere into those plans. He'd dedicated his life to breast-cancer research and nothing more.

Marrying Taylor had been rash—the effects of alcohol and Las Vegas craziness—and wasn't at all like his normal self. Women were temporary in his life, not permanent figures. He preferred it that way.

A divorce sounded perfect. His marriage would be one of those "what happens in Vegas stays in Vegas" kind of things.

Thank goodness she didn't harbor any delusions of happily-ever-after or sappy romance. They'd chalk last night up to alcohol and a major lapse of judgment.

Maybe there really was something about Vegas that made people throw caution to the wind and act outside their norm. Or maybe it had been the smiley little elfish limo driver, who'd kept puffing peppermint spray into the car, telling them they were at the wedding chapel that had made the idea seem feasible. Had the spray been some type of drug?

"Good." Taylor's chin lifted a couple of notches. "Then we're agreed this was a mistake and we can get a divorce or an annulment or whatever one does in these circumstances."

"I'll call my lawyer first thing Monday morning." Relieved that she was being sensible about calling a spade a spade and correcting their mistake, he pushed the room-service cart over next to the bed and stared down at a woman who'd taken him to sexual heights he'd never experienced before. Maybe that peppermint stuff really had been some kind of aphrodisiac.

Even with her haughty expression, she was pretty with

her long blond hair tumbled over her milky shoulders and her lips swollen from his kisses. Until the night before he'd never seen her hair down. He liked it. A lot.

He liked her a lot. Always had. He'd wanted her from afar for way too long. Despite the whole marriage fiasco, he still wanted her. Even more than he had prior to having kissed her addictive mouth. She'd tasted of candy canes, joy and magic. Kissing her had made him feel like a kid on Christmas morning who'd gotten exactly what he'd always wanted.

Which was saying a lot for a man who hadn't celebrated Christmas since he was twelve years old.

"Now that that's settled, there's no reason we can't enjoy the rest of the weekend. Let's eat up before this gets cold."

The covers still clasped to her all the way up to her neck, she crossed her arms over her chest. Her eyes were narrow green slits of annoyance. "Don't act as if we're suddenly friends because we both want a divorce. We're not and we won't be enjoying the rest of the weekend. At least, not the way you mean."

"Fine. We won't enjoy the rest of the weekend." He wasn't going to argue with her. "But we're not strangers." Ignoring her I-can't-stand-you glare and his irritation at how she was treating him as if he had mange, he lifted the lid off one of the dishes he'd ordered and began buttering a slice of toast. "I've been working with you for around a year."

"You see me at work." She watched what he did with great interest. "That doesn't make us friends. Neither does last night."

She had to be starved. While satisfying one hunger, they'd worked up another. He'd ordered a little of everything because he hadn't known what she liked. Other than coffee. Often at the clinic, he saw her sipping on a mug of coffee as if the stuff were ambrosia. Funny how often he'd catch himself watching for her to take that first sip, how he'd smile at the pleasure on her face once she had. He'd put pleasure on her face the night before that had blown away anything he'd ever seen, anything he'd ever experienced.

"You make your point." He sat down on the bed and waved a piece of buttered toast in front of her, liking how her gaze followed the offering. "But as we're in agreement that we made a mistake, one we are rectifying, I don't see why we can't be friends and make the most out of a bad situation."

Scowling, she shot her gaze back to his. "You and I will never be friends."

She grabbed his toast and took a bite, closed her eyes and sighed a noise that made him want to push her back on the bed and, friends or not, taste her all over again.

Perhaps she'd prefer it if he told her how much he was enjoying how she'd just licked crumbs from her pretty pink lips? How much, now that he knew disentangling himself from their impromptu marriage wasn't going to be a problem, he was anticipating making love to her again, because for all her blustering he wasn't blind. She'd looked at him with more hunger than she had the toast. Whether she wanted to admit it or not, she was as affected by him as he was her. They had phenomenal chemistry.

She leaned toward the tray, got a knife and a packet of strawberry jam, then nodded while she spread the pink mixture on what was left of her toast. Not an easy task because she refused to let go of where she clutched the bed covers, which seemed a bit ridiculous to him since he'd seen every inch of her. Seen, touched, tasted.

Slade swallowed the lump forming in his throat and mentally ordered one not to form beneath his towel. "In case you need reminding, we had a good time last night."

"I didn't."

"Don't lie." He'd been there. She hadn't faked that, couldn't have faked her responses, and he wouldn't let her pretend she had. "Yes, you did."

"Okay," she conceded with a great deal of sarcasm.

"You're good in bed. Anyone can be good if they get lots of practice and we both know you've had lots of practice."

"Lots of practice?" He hadn't lived the life of a monk, but he didn't go around picking up random women every night either. Sure, he never committed, but the women he spent time with knew the score. He wasn't the marrying kind and avoided women who were. "You want to discuss my past sex life?"

"Not really." Her face squished, then paled. "Although I guess we should discuss diseases and such."

He arched his brow. "You have a disease?"

"No." She sounded horrified enough that he knew she was telling the truth. They should have discussed all this the night before. And birth control. Because for the first time in his life he hadn't used a condom. Because for the first time in his life he'd been making love to his *wife*.

Slade's throat tightened. He'd not only gotten married the night before but he'd had sex without a condom. How stupid could he have been?

Was that why the sex had been so good? Because they'd not had a rubber barrier between them? Because they'd been flesh to flesh? He didn't think so. There had been something more, something special about kissing Taylor.

Besides, they'd used a condom the first time. It had been their subsequent trips to heaven that had been without one. He'd only had the one condom in his wallet and they'd still been high under the Las Vegas night air—or whatever foolishness had lowered their inhibitions.

"Do you?" she asked, sounding somewhere between terrified and hopeful his answer would be the right one.

"I haven't specifically gone for testing recently." There hadn't been a need. He had never had sex without protection before her and didn't engage in any other high-risk behaviors. "It's been a year or so since my last checkup, but I do donate blood routinely and have always checked normal."

His answer didn't appease her and she eyed him suspiciously. "When was the last time you donated?"

"About two months ago."

Relief washed over her face. "No letter telling you about any abnormal findings?"

He shook his head. "No such letter. What about you?"

Her gaze didn't quite meet his. "I've only been with one man and that was years ago during medical school. I've been checked a couple of times since then. I'm clean."

As unreasonable as it was since he was no saint and they were going to end their marriage as soon as possible, the thought of Taylor being with anyone else irked him. A surge of jealousy had his fingers flexing and his brain going on hiatus.

"He didn't have to marry you to have sex with you?"

CHAPTER TWO

SLADE INSTANTLY REGRETTED his sarcastic question, especially when, with a pale face and watery eyes, Taylor glanced down at the plain gold band he'd put on her hand the night before.

"No, Kyle didn't marry me, but I did believe he was going to spend the rest of his life loving me. Silly me."

The fact that she'd been heartbroken by the jerk rankled Slade. Good thing she didn't want this marriage any more than he did. He'd hate to think he'd hurt her like that fool had. Regardless of what the future held for them, he didn't want to cause Taylor any pain. That much he knew. "What happened?"

She shrugged and the sheet slipped off one shoulder to drape mid-upper-arm. "He didn't marry me or spend the rest of his life loving me. End of story."

Hardly, but he wouldn't push. Such sorrow laced her words that his chest squeezed tighter. "I'm sorry."

"I'm not." Masking her emotions behind an indifferent expression he suspected she'd perfected over the years since her breakup with the guy, Taylor picked up a spoon and scooped up a mouthful of eggs. "He was an arrogant jerk."

Her lips were wrapped around the spoon and another jolt of jealousy hit him as she slowly pulled the utensil from her mouth.

She picked up a strawberry and bit into the juicy fruit. "Mmm. That's good."

"Speaking of good…" He watched her pop the rest of the berry into her mouth and lick the juice from her fingers, and struggled with the desire to do some licking of his own. "Last night really was spectacular, apart from the whole getting-married thing."

She met his gaze, nodded, then deflated. "Oh, Slade, what have we done?"

Hearing her say his name caused flashbacks from the night before. Until then, he'd never heard her say his first name. He liked the sound. "We got married, but we can correct that. We will correct that. As soon as legally possible."

"It's crazy that we got married. Why did we do that? We aren't in love, barely know each other and I don't even like you."

He gave a wry grin. "All this time I just thought you were waiting on me to win you over to my way of thinking."

"Professionally maybe, but not romantically."

"Professionally, I'm a good oncologist."

"You are." She winced. "I didn't mean it like that."

"Then what did you mean?"

"Just that I always thought you were a flirt and didn't take life seriously."

"I take my job very seriously." His work was the most important thing in his life and always would be. "I care a great deal for my patients and like to think I provide them the best care possible."

"You do. It's just that…" Her voice trailed off.

"It's just what?"

"I guess I let your personal life influence how I viewed you professionally."

"What do you know of my personal life?"

Her face reddened. "Not much. Just gossip really."

"Not that you should believe gossip, but what do the gossips say?"

"That you date a lot of different women."

"You think I shouldn't?"

She sighed and looked somewhere between disgusted and desperate. "What I think about your personal life doesn't matter. We'll get a divorce and no one ever need know about any of this."

Thankful that she was so practical about the whole thing, Slade nodded. "Agreed. We'll figure the legalities out on Monday and end this as painlessly as possible."

She eyed him, then gave a hopeful half smile. "Maybe we'll get lucky and there's some kind of 'just kidding, I've changed my mind because I was stupid in Vegas clause.'"

Thank goodness Slade felt the same as she did. They'd made a horrible mistake, knew it and would make the best of a bad situation.

Not that she could believe he'd married her.

The man was gorgeous, amazing in bed, could have any woman he wanted and usually did, according to her female coworkers who loved to discuss the handsome oncologist's love life latest. Why would he have married her? Taylor was admittedly a stick-in-the-mud, boring homebody. Her idea of fun was a good book while soaking in a bubble bath or playing with Gracie. Her ideal life would bore him to tears. No confetti and blow horns anywhere in her reality or her ideal future.

From what she knew about Slade, they couldn't be more opposite.

Opposites attract.

She winced at the inner voice in her head playing devil's advocate. Okay, so she'd admit she wanted to rip Slade's towel off and have that encore performance. Not that she did anything more than wrap the sheet around her, grab the cup of coffee from the tray, and, head held high, strut into the bathroom to take her shower.

Of course, that only reminded her that his naked body

had been under this hot stream earlier and had she wakened in time she could have joined him. Her husband.

What a joke.

But right now she had to get her act together, because they were presenting to a group of oncologists, pharmacists, marketing representatives and others on the benefits of a new cancer-fighting drug they'd been researching.

At some point today she should probably tell Slade that not only had he become a husband the night before, he'd also become the stepfather of a precious six-year-old little girl.

She winced.

Yeah, that might shock Slade enough to have him scrambling around in hopes of finding a twenty-four-hour Vegas divorce court.

Although she had a photo of Gracie on her desk at work, she doubted Slade had ever been inside the room, that he'd ever had reason to be in her personal office. Yes, they worked in the same multifloor cancer clinic. But prior to their being chosen to go to this conference to discuss the research being done at their facility, they'd not really interacted except when he'd sent her running by asking her out.

Because she avoided men like Slade.

Had for years.

The last time she hadn't, she'd ended up pregnant and alone.

Nausea hit her. After their first time she and Slade hadn't used birth control. He'd only had the one condom, and they'd been too delirious to acknowledge the ramifications of unprotected sex.

How stupid was she? Was he?

The timing in her menstrual cycle wasn't right for pregnancy, but she wasn't so foolish as to think it wasn't possible.

Her hand went to her bare belly. Was she? Had she and Slade made a baby? Dampness covered her skin that had nothing to do with the shower water. She loved Gracie with all her heart, would do anything for her precious daughter, but she'd never planned to have more children. Not without finding a man who met all her criteria for Mr. Right, which included what kind of father he'd be to Gracie.

Then again, she'd never planned to get married to a man she barely knew either, and she'd done that.

Her parents would be so proud. Ha. Not. Her actions this weekend would just once again affirm their disappointment in her.

She finished rinsing her body, then stepped out of the shower and eyed the half-empty cup of coffee.

She picked up the cup and, with great sadness, poured the lukewarm liquid down the sink drain.

No more coffee or anything else that wasn't healthy for a pregnant woman until she knew for sure one way or the other that she and Slade hadn't created a new little life.

Slade leaned back in his chair and watched the impressive woman woo the crowd with her smiles and witty sense of humor.

Taylor went through the slide presentation she'd put together on the data their oncology clinic, Nashville Cancer Care, had collected on Interallon, a new experimental cancer-fighting drug they'd been successfully administering as part of a larger nationwide research trial. Remission rates of metastatic breast cancer had increased by 40 percent in patients who'd received the trial medication over current treatment modalities. They were hopeful FDA approval would be soon so the medication could be administered more widely.

Taylor pushed back a stray strand of pale blond hair behind her ear and pointed a laser at the current slide, referring to a particular set of data.

He'd slid his fingers through that soft, long hair last night. Not that you could tell just how long or lush her hair was with the way she had it harshly swept up. Neither could you tell how gorgeous her big green eyes were behind those ridiculous black-rimmed glasses she wore. Definitely you couldn't tell how hot and passionate her body was beneath her prim and proper gray pantsuit and blazer.

She epitomized a professional businesswoman presenting data to a crowd of health-care professionals who couldn't possibly appreciate how amazing she was.

Slade scanned the crowd, noticing several of the men watching her with a gleam in their eyes. Well, maybe some of them did see just how amazing she was, but he pitied them. She was his. His wife.

He couldn't believe he'd gone that far.

He usually had no problems with women, but Taylor had always been different. For months he'd not been able to convince her to give him the time of day and he had tried. Repeatedly, he'd struck up conversations only to have her end them and avoid him.

She made a comment, misspoke a word and poked fun at herself, getting a laugh from their audience. Slade skimmed the crowd, noticing several of the men seemed to be further enchanted by the woman on stage.

Green slushed through his veins, clogging the oxygen flow to his brain. Had to be since he sure wasn't thinking straight because his brain—or was it just his male ego?—was screaming, *Mine. Mine. Mine.*

"Now…" She flashed another smile at the crowd, pulling them further under her spell. "I'll turn the podium over to Dr. Slade Sain to present specific case studies and then we'll field any questions together."

They walked past each other as he took the podium and she returned to sit in the seat next to his at a table that had been set up at the front of the auditorium. He tried to meet her gaze, to smile at her and tell her what a great job she'd done, but she kept her gaze averted, purposely not looking at him.

Which annoyed Slade.

He stewed all the way to the podium and then did something almost as stupid as slipping a golden band around a woman's finger when he had nothing to offer her but more broken dreams.

"Ladies and gentlemen, give my wife a round of applause for the great job she just did."

Taylor's face paled.

Slade's face probably did, too. What had he just done?

Several of the people in the audience who knew them gasped in surprise. A few called out their congratulations.

When their gazes met, Taylor looked annoyed, but then she pasted on a smile for the crowd.

Their colleagues and class attendees settled down and, despite the horror bubbling in his stomach that he'd just made their mistake public, Slade got serious. He believed in the benefits of Interallon and wanted others to have the opportunity to significantly benefit from the still-experimental medication. Despite whatever was going on in their personal lives, it was his and Taylor's job to educate their colleagues, to get others involved in the medication trials, as the pharmaceutical company pushed to have the FDA expedite approval.

He went over their case studies, answered questions, then pointed to one of their colleagues whose hand was raised with a question. The doctor had started out with him and Taylor the night before, but they'd ditched him and a handful of others when they'd left in the limo.

"Sorry to change the subject off Interallon, but when did you and Dr. Anderson get married?"

"Last night." Slade glanced toward Taylor. Her green eyes flashed with anger beneath her glasses, but she kept a smile on her lovely face. No doubt he was going to get a tongue-lashing when the presentation finished. He deserved one. He wanted to scream and yell at himself for his stupid remark, too. "Next question."

The man raised his hand again and spoke before Slade could call on another person. "You and Dr. Anderson got married last night? When you left dinner, you got married?"

Taylor stood, walked over to the podium, and took the microphone. "Dr. Ryan, you'll understand if Dr. Sain and I request personal questions be saved for a later, more appropriate time. Right now, we prefer questions regarding Interallon and the success our clinic and the other clinics involved in the trials taking place are having with this phenomenal resource in our battle against a horrific disease."

Put in his place, the man nodded. Taylor immediately called on another person and fielded a question about the medication being used in conjunction with currently available treatments.

"At this time, the studies using Interallon in conjunction with other cancer-fighting modalities are just starting to take place. Nashville Cancer Care will be heading up one of those trials early next year."

Another flurry of questions filled the remaining time and no one brought up their nuptials again until after the class was over. Several of their colleagues shook their hands, patted their backs and gave them congratulations.

"I didn't see that one coming," Dr. Ryan commented, looking back and forth between them. "I didn't even know you two were seeing each other."

Slade narrowed his gaze at the other man. Cole Ryan had been one of the men eyeing Taylor on stage as if she was a piece of candy to be devoured. A growl gurgled in Slade's throat, but he managed to keep it low.

Taylor closed her laptop and picked up a file folder with her notes inside. "I prefer to keep my personal life private. Obviously, Dr. Sain and I disagree on that particular issue."

"Dr. Sain?" Ryan chuckled, then slapped Slade on the back again. "Your wife calls you Dr. Sain?"

Slade glanced at Taylor's scowl, the stiff set to her shoulders and the tight line of her mouth. He was an idiot. He deserved her anger. He didn't even know why he'd made the stupid announcement. Other than the fact that he'd been overcome with jealousy. "When she's upset."

"Trouble in paradise already. That's a Vegas wedding for you." The man laughed again, not realizing just how much he was getting on Slade's nerves. Odd, as he usually liked the doctor, who also practiced in Nashville.

"Well, congrats anyway." Cole gave them a wry look. "For however long it lasts."

Slade packed up his briefcase and followed Taylor from the conference room and down the long hallway that led out into the hotel's main lobby.

Ignoring the lush Christmas decorations and colorful slot machines scattered around the huge lobby, Taylor didn't say a word directly to him until they were alone in the elevator. Then she rounded on him, opened her mouth to speak, then stopped, closed her eyes in disgust and took a deep breath. When she opened her eyes again, anger still flickered there. "How dare you make that little announcement during our presentation?"

"I shouldn't have said anything."

"You made a joke of our presentation," she accused, practically snapping at him.

"No, I didn't." He would never intentionally do anything to take away from the importance of Interallon and the results they were getting with the medication.

"Yes, you did. Rather than paying attention to what you were saying, half the people in the room were busy Tweeting that we'd gotten married."

"You're exaggerating." He hoped she was exaggerating.

"Really?" She dug in her bag and held up her phone. "This thing has been buzzing like crazy since you made your little comment. Forget the fact that our marriage is a sham, but how dare you make a mockery of my work?"

"That's not what I was doing." Guilt hit him. She was right. They were getting a divorce as soon as it could be arranged. The fewer people who knew of their mistake the better. He'd been out of line to say anything.

"That's exactly what you were doing." She looked as if

she'd like to hit him, but instead just gritted her teeth and made a sound that was somewhere between a growl and a sigh.

"You're right," he agreed with sincerity and regret. "I shouldn't have said what I did. I'm sorry, Taylor."

That seemed to take the steam out of her argument, as if she hadn't expected him to apologize. Rather than say more she just rolled her eyes upward, her long lashes brushing the lenses of her heavy-framed glasses.

The elevator beeped and the door slid open. She practically ran out. Slade followed, his eyes never leaving her as she marched to her door, dug in her bag for her room key card, then slid the card into the slot. He got there just as she pushed open the door and went inside, not waiting for him.

Slade hesitated only a second, then caught the door before it closed, and went inside to try to repair the damage he'd done.

He wasn't very good at this husband thing.

Good thing he didn't plan to be one for long.

CHAPTER THREE

TAYLOR GLANCED AROUND her hotel room and wanted to scream. Those weren't her things.

They were Slade's things.

Her blood boiled. How could he have been so stupid as to have announced that they'd married? She'd just wanted to have a quiet quickie divorce. She had not wanted anyone to know. Now everyone knew. Right before Christmas. Ugh.

She threw her bag down on her bed, wincing when she recalled her laptop was inside. She clicked on her phone to see who the latest text was from. Her parents? No doubt they'd hear of her latest "major life mistake" soon enough.

The text was from Nina. Great. Had her friend said anything to Gracie? She prayed not. No way did she want Gracie to know what an idiot she had for a mother.

Married in Vegas to a virtual stranger. Brilliant example she was setting for her impressionable young daughter. Shame on her. No doubt her parents would remind her of that over and over.

I just read that you married Slade Sain! Is that true? Hello, girlfriend, have you been holding out on me? I didn't know you two were an item and I'm your best friend!

"We need to talk."

Clutching her phone, Taylor spun at Slade's words. "You need to get out of my room."

"This is our room."

"Get out," she repeated.

"Taylor." He raked his fingers through his hair. "I'm sorry I messed up. You're right that I shouldn't have said anything. Unfortunately, I did and I can't take the words back."

"I didn't want anyone to know I married you!"

Something akin to hurt flickered across his face. "Not that I want to be married any more than you do, but am I such a loser that you're ashamed of me?"

Surprised that he sincerely looked offended, Taylor sank onto the foot of the bed and sighed. "This is crazy. I don't want to argue with you, Slade. I don't want to say hurtful things. I don't want you here. I don't want to be married to you. I don't want anyone to know. I don't want to face our colleagues at this dinner tonight, knowing that they're going to be watching us."

"That's a lot of 'I don't wants,'" he mused, his voice gentler than before. He knelt down on the floor in front of her. His eyes searched hers. "What is it you do want, Taylor?"

Although he wasn't touching her, his nearness made her insides tremble. Probably from disgust that she'd married him. "To forget this ever happened and to not be married to you of all people."

"Of all people? Ouch."

"I'm sorry if I'm wounding your ego, but don't pretend that it's anything more than that," she pointed out, wishing he'd move away from her. How was she supposed to not look at him when he was right there, kneeling in front of her? "Yes, we had sex together and it was good. But we aren't in love and we won't ever be. This was a mistake and what's worse is that it's now a public mistake." Oh, how she hated that anyone knew how big a mistake she'd made. "And above all else I don't want Gracie to find out."

Confusion furrowed his brows. "Who's Gracie?"

She might as well tell him. "My daughter."

Shock registered on his face and for a moment she thought his knees were going to give way. "You have a daughter?"

"Yes, I have a daughter." She snorted. Just as well Slade wasn't the man of her dreams, because his reaction to the news of Gracie would have killed any chance he had.

Face a little blanched, he shook his head. "You don't have a kid."

He sounded so confident in his immediate response that Taylor wanted to laugh. Only she wasn't feeling very amused at the moment. She was feeling crowded with him so close to her and annoyed at his reaction.

"Sure I do." She narrowed her gaze, hoping he'd take the hint at how much she disliked him. "Perhaps you noticed the stretch marks along my hips last night when we were..." Her cheeks heated. Crazy after the things they'd done the night before that she couldn't bring herself to say the word *sex*.

But whereas she was annoyed, his expression remained shocked. "You have a beautiful body, Taylor." His tone was as gentle as it had been before, but there was a dazed look to his eyes. "And no more stretch marks than other women have with fluctuations in weight of a few pounds."

He would know.

Ugh. She hated it that her mind went to him with other women. But, then, he did go through women just as fast as Kyle had, so why wouldn't her mind go there? He was a player. A player she had married and was going to divorce.

"Puh-lease." She didn't even attempt to hide her sarcasm. "I've given birth. I know my body changes. I don't know what game you're playing, but get real."

"You have a beautiful body, Taylor," he repeated, so matter-of-fact that something cracked deep inside even if his words only meant he hadn't really looked at her.

"The body of a woman who has had a baby. If you'd paid attention last night, you'd have realized that."

He ignored her snap, stood and paced across the room. When he turned to look at her, he didn't meet her eyes. "When?"

"Gracie is six."

The skin on his face pulled tight. His jaw worked back and forth in a slow grind. "The guy in medical school?"

She nodded and couldn't hold in her bitterness. How dared Slade look at her with accusation in his eyes? He had no right to judge her! "Give the man a prize. Of course he's Gracie's father. I told you he was the only man I'd ever been with."

"There are other ways women become mothers, Taylor," he pointed out, his voice level and patient, even though color stained his cheeks at her outburst. "A strong, successful woman like yourself may have decided to have a child and sought a fertility clinic, for all I know."

Strong, successful woman? Ha, what she really wanted to do at the moment was curl up into a ball and cry. How strong and successful was that?

"Because, like I've said, you don't know me. This just proves my point."

His jaw flexed again. "A point I tried to correct on numerous occasions, but you didn't want to let me know you."

"Of course I don't want to let you know me. You've ruined my life." She was crying now. She didn't want to cry, but from the moment he'd made his comment about his "wife" during their presentation and her phone had started vibrating in her bag, she'd wanted to cry. There was no more holding the tears back. Yep, strong and successful, that was so her. Just ask her parents.

"Please, don't cry, Taylor." He sounded almost as lost as she felt. "I want to make you smile, not cry."

The last thing she wanted was to cry in front of him, but she couldn't make the tears stop. She cried for her parents and how embarrassed they were going to be by her. Again. She cried for Gracie and how her mother's moment of stupidity would affect her. And she cried for herself, that she'd been so easily led astray after six years of living an exemplary life.

"Tell me what I can do to make things better."

"Go away," she immediately informed him.

He stared at her for long moments then gave a slight nod of his head. "I'm sorry I've upset you, Taylor. I'll go for now. I have a meeting at noon anyway, but I will be back later to change for dinner. I hope you'll be ready to talk, because whether we like it or not we are married, people do know and we need a game plan on how best to deal with this so that it has the least negative impact on both our lives."

"I heard a rumor today."

Slade winced. He should have known better than to answer the phone when he'd seen who was calling. "Hey, Dad."

"Is what I'm hearing true, son?"

"Depends on what you've been hearing."

"You married?"

How did he answer his father? The best man he'd ever known through and through. A man who cherished the bonds of marriage, a man who had lost his precious wife, Slade's mother, to cancer, and carried that bond still in his heart, despite the fact he'd remarried several years back to a good woman.

Slade couldn't lie to his father. "Guess some rumors are true."

Silence ticked over the phone line.

"Have to admit I'm surprised," his father said slowly. More silence. "She pregnant?"

Slade's face heated. Not that he could blame his father for asking. Everyone who really knew him knew he'd never planned to marry, that he had dedicated his life to medicine, to finding a cure for a disease he hated.

"Not that I know of. She does have a kid, though." Hadn't that one been a shocker? Not only had he married but he'd also become an instant father. Not that it really mattered. He wasn't likely to meet Taylor's daughter. They'd divorce, pretend as if none of this had ever happened, and that would be the end of their Vegas mistake.

Which was exactly what needed to happen, so why did the image of Taylor's tears flash through his mind and make him wish life was different? That he was different?

Then again, hadn't he learned at twelve years old that wishes didn't come true? If they did, his mother would still be alive because he'd wished more than any kid had ever wished. He was sure of it.

More silence.

"For a man who just got married, you don't sound very happy. You okay, son?"

Okay? Again, the image of Taylor's tear-streaked face popped into his mind. No, he wasn't okay. He'd married a woman he wanted physically, cared for as a person and whom he didn't want to damage emotionally. "I'm fine."

"You're not in some kind of trouble, are you?" Worry weighed heavily in his father's words. "This is just so unexpected."

Slade could almost laugh. "I'm not in trouble, Dad."

At least, not the kind his father meant.

"Well, then, congratulations."

Congratulations. Because he'd gotten married. And become a father. Why did his tie feel as if it was strangling him?

He couldn't even respond to his father's comment.

"She must be something special," his dad continued.

Images from the night before flashed through Slade's mind, images of sharing laughter with Taylor, of holding her hand as they'd climbed into the limo to leave the hotel, of kissing her in the back of the limo, of how his heart had pounded in his chest as he'd slid a ring onto her finger and promised to have and hold her forever…

Maybe he was in trouble, because as much as he didn't want to be married, didn't want to think about the fact she was a mother, he did want Taylor in his life.

If only she weren't so complicated. If only they hadn't gotten married.

"Taylor is special," he admitted, then realized just how much he'd revealed in his three softly spoken words.

"I'm glad to hear that. After your mother died you avoided getting close to anyone. I'm glad you've met some-one worth the risk."

Slade's ribs threatened to crush the contents of his chest they constricted so tightly. He hadn't avoided getting close to anyone. He'd just made a conscious decision to dedicate his life to finding a cure for breast cancer. His father didn't understand that. Maybe no one could. But to Slade, doing all he could to prevent others from going through what his family had was his number-one life priority.

"Dad, I hate to cut you short." Not really a lie. He loved his father, enjoyed talking to him normally, just not today, not when he was reeling from the past twenty-four hours, from the fact he'd woken up with a wife and a kid. "But I'm on my way to my dream job interview with Grandview Pharmaceuticals." A dream job that would give him every opportunity of achieving his number-one life priority. "I'll give you a call next week when I'm back in Nashville."

"Hello, my darling, how was school today?" Taylor said into the phone to her daughter. The first rays of happiness were shining that day.

"Good," the most precious voice in the world answered. "Aunt Nina said I was very smart."

Although she was no blood relation, Gracie had called Taylor's best friend "Aunt" for as long as Taylor could re-member.

"Aunt Nina is right. You are a smart girl. And a very pretty one."

Gracie giggled. "You always say that."

"Because it's true."

"I miss you, Mommy." Gracie's voice sounded somewhere between sad and pouty. Taylor could just picture her daughter's expression, see the sadness in the green eyes that were so similar to her own.

"I miss you, too." More than words could convey.

"When are you coming home?" Gracie demanded.

"I'll be flying home tomorrow evening. You and Aunt Nina are picking me up from the airport."

"Are you bringing me a prize? Aunt Nina said if I was good while you were gone that I'd get a present."

"Aunt Nina said that, did she? So close to Christmas? Well, I'm sure if she said that, then she's right."

Gracie talked to her a few minutes more, then handed the phone to Nina.

"She's something else, isn't she?" Nina immediately said into the phone.

"I hope she's not been too much trouble," Taylor told her best friend.

"Are you kidding me? I've loved having her here. She's helped me decorate my house and you know me, I'm one of those who never has things done the week after Thanksgiving. This year, I'm way ahead of the game, and she and I have had a blast getting everything done."

Taylor understood. Gracie was a blast and loved Christmas almost as much as her mother did. No doubt the little girl had garlands and lights strung all over Nina's apartment.

"Good. When they told me I would be going on this trip, my first thoughts were what I'd do about Gracie. I've never left her before."

"Are you sure your first thoughts weren't about getting an early Christmas package from a certain sexy oncologist?

Or perhaps the two of you just got carried away beneath some Vegas mistletoe?"

Taylor sighed. She had known Nina would ask about Slade. Especially since she hadn't answered a single text message from Nina or any of her other friends and colleagues. What was she supposed to say? *Yes, I messed up again. It's what I'm good at when it comes to the opposite sex.*

"You might as well tell me, because you know you're going to. Best friend, remember?"

"I remember."

"So what's up with you becoming Mrs. Dr. Sexy?"

Taylor winced. "Please tell me you didn't ask me that in front of Gracie."

"She's watching her favorite television program and is totally oblivious to what I'm saying."

"Don't count on it. She picks up on a lot more than people give her credit for."

"Fine, I'll walk into the kitchen." There was a short pause. "Now, tell me if what I read was true."

"It's true."

Nina squealed. "You and Dr. Sain got married? How romantic! Tell me everything."

"There wasn't anything romantic about it." Which wasn't exactly true. Drunk or not, he'd been sweet when he'd slid the wedding ring onto her finger, had lifted her hand and placed a kiss over the gold band. Just the memory goosebumped her skin.

"You got married to the sexiest man we know and there wasn't anything romantic about it?"

She sank her teeth into her lower lip. "Not really."

"Which means there was at least something romantic going on," Nina concluded. "Hubba-hubba. This is huge. You got married. I can't believe it."

"That makes two of us."

"This is so unlike you. You're, like, never spontaneous. I

just…" Nina paused and Taylor could just imagine her friend shaking her head while she tried to make sense of what was being said. "So, tell me the details. How in the world did you and Dr. Sain get married?"

"A bunch of us had dinner, went to watch a Christmas show and then I ended up in a limo with Slade. We drove to a cheesy year-round Christmas wedding chapel and exchanged vows. Alcohol was involved."

Nina moaned. "Please tell me it wasn't a drive-through ceremony."

"It wasn't." Although if it had been, would it really have mattered? "Santa Claus married us."

"Santa?"

"An impersonator, but, yes, Santa. There were even elves snapping pictures and throwing fake snow at us." Ugh. Taylor rubbed her temple. "What am I going to do, Nina? I got married last night."

"Celebrate the fact that you married the hottest guy around and will be the envy of every female at the clinic?"

"I'm serious."

"Me, too. So, how was he?"

"Nina!"

"That good, huh?"

"That good," Taylor agreed, unable to lie. "Better than any man should be." Better than she'd thought any man could be. He'd set her body aflame and made her ache for more. "But I can't stay married to him."

"Why not?"

"We never should have gotten married in the first place. We were under the influence and made a huge mistake. Besides, he is about as opposite from what I want in a man as possible."

"You want ugly, not sexy and not good in bed?"

"You know what I mean." Would her temple please stop throbbing?

"Fine. I know what you mean, but you did get married.

Show a little more enthusiasm, please. Didn't you joke last year after Christmas that you should have asked Santa for a man? Well, girl, you must have been at the top of the nice list this year for Santa to have delivered Slade Sain."

She did recall joking with Nina that she should have asked Santa for a man. She didn't want to be alone, raising Gracie without a father. But she'd much rather that than to have let the wrong man into her life. She sighed.

"We're going to get a divorce just as soon as it can be arranged." She twisted the gold band on her left hand. Why hadn't she taken it off? Why did it feel seared to her very being?

"Too bad."

Taylor pulled back her phone to stare at it. "I can't believe you said that. I made a horrible mistake last night. Can you imagine what my parents are going to say?"

"Who cares what they say, Taylor? You can't keep trying to make up for disappointing them by getting pregnant out of wedlock. These are modern times. Women have kids without being married. You finished school and have made a great life for you and Gracie. If your parents can't see what a wonderful woman you are, then phooey on them."

In theory, Taylor knew her friend was right. In her heart, she hated to disappoint her parents again. They were devoutly religious, had the perfect marriage, couldn't understand how she'd let herself become pregnant out of wedlock and although they loved Gracie, they'd never let Taylor forget how disappointed they'd been.

"I know you, Taylor," Nina continued. "I'm not sure how you and Slade ended up married. There must have been some major Christmas magic in the air last night. But quit stressing and enjoy the rest of your honeymoon before planning your divorce. Reality will set in soon enough."

"I'm not on a honeymoon and reality set in first thing this morning."

"Technically, you are on your honeymoon," Nina pointed out. "You got married last night."

Taylor dropped backward onto the bed. "Crap. You're right. I'm so stupid."

"You're the least stupid person I know."

Taylor just groaned.

"Obviously, there was something between you two last night that triggered the 'I do's,'" Nina pointed out in her ever-optimistic way. "You married a superhot guy who you had really great sex with and now he's your husband. Why not quit worrying about the details and the pending legal 'I don't's and just enjoy your honeymoon?"

If only life were that easy. "You don't mean that."

"Why wouldn't I? You never do anything for yourself, Taylor. You're always working or doing things for Gracie. For the next twenty-four hours don't worry about anyone but yourself. The act is done. You're married and on your honeymoon with a hunk. Take advantage of that, of him and his skills. What's going to happen in the future is going to happen regardless of whether or not you grasp hold of what life's presented to you on a silver platter. Or, in this case, what Santa's wrapped up in a pretty bow. I say go for it, work off some long-overdue steam, and make some memories before going your separate ways."

Ugh. Her friend almost made sense. Almost. "You're not helping."

"Sure I am. I'm just not saying what your determined-to-be-a-prude ears want to hear."

"I hate it when you're right."

Nina squealed again. "So, you're going to do it? You're going to let your hair down and rock Dr. Sain's world?"

She wasn't so sure she could rock his world, but he had seemed to enjoy the night before. They had been hot.

"I'm not sure I know how to let loose anymore," she admitted, positive it was true. She enjoyed life, but all her free time did revolve around Gracie. "And I didn't say you were right that I should let my hair down. Just that what you were saying wasn't what I wanted to hear."

"You want me to tell you that you should hightail it back home and file for divorce without indulging in some fun with your husband first?"

File for divorce. Pressure squeezed her heart. People in her family didn't divorce. They didn't get pregnant out of wedlock and they didn't marry virtual strangers in Vegas and they didn't divorce. That was her family.

But she would be three for three because she would be filing for divorce. To pretend otherwise was ridiculous. She and Slade had suffered lapses of judgement, clouded by lust and alcohol. That much she could admit to. She'd wanted him last night. When he'd kissed her, she'd melted and forgotten everything but him.

"I'm waiting for an answer."

Taylor's grip on her cell phone tightened. "I'm a mother, Nina. Regardless of what I want, I can't just go around indulging in fun whenever I want to. It's not that I don't want to indulge in fun, because I do." Oh, how she wanted to imbibe more of Slade. "He was amazing. An affair with him would be amazing, but I need to end this without doing anything that might complicate things."

"Too late. Things are already complicated."

Taylor's gaze shot to the open hotel room door and the man who stood there. Crap. When had he opened the door and how much had he overheard?

"Sorry, Nina, but I've got to go." Her gaze latched on to Slade's and she refused to look away even when that's what she wanted to do. How was it he made her feel so on edge with just a look? "My husband just walked in."

CHAPTER FOUR

FRUSTRATED, SLADE STARED at the woman lying on the bed. Clicking off her phone, Taylor slowly rose to a sitting position. Which was exactly where he'd left her.

She'd left the hotel room, though. He'd gone to a presentation, had sensed her sneaking into the meeting room and had turned to catch her sliding into a seat in the back of the auditorium. When the meeting had ended, he'd glanced her way. She'd been gone.

He'd forced himself to go to all the programs he'd marked on his agenda, even though he'd had a difficult time staying focused on what the presenters had been saying. At noon, he'd had an interview with Grandview Pharmaceuticals, the company that owned Interallon and that was renowned for their headway in the fight against cancer.

John Cordova, the older man who'd interviewed him, had commented on how they needed someone dependable, someone able to make long-term commitments, to see things through, to fill the position. The man had then congratulated him on his recent marriage.

Slade had withheld the fact that his marriage wasn't a long-term commitment but a mistake. He'd gotten the impression that a divorce so quickly following his marriage wouldn't have won him any brownie points in Cordova's eyes.

His phone call with his father played through his head.

His father was going to be so disappointed in him when he told him the truth.

His temple throbbed ever so slightly. He found himself wishing he could lie on the bed beside Taylor, talk to her about the interview, about his goals and dreams, about his mother and how much he missed her, about the concern in his father's voice and how he hadn't had the heart to tell him that his marriage was over before it even started either. He wanted to talk with her the way they had the night before because talking to her, being with her, had felt so right.

Too bad Taylor was staring at him as if he were a serial killer.

Last night had been different. When she'd looked at him, he'd seen something more. That something more had triggered some kind of insanity. She'd wanted to have sex with him, and that knowledge had shot madness into his veins. She'd challenged him with her condition about marriage and, gazing into her eyes, he'd lost his mind and the ability to walk away from the temptation she'd offered.

He had the feeling that before all was said and done, his insanity was going to cost him a lot more than he'd bargained for.

She cleared her throat, reminding him that he had been staring at her for way too long.

"I need to change for the dinner program."

A semiformal conference farewell that was more socializing than anything else.

"That's fine." She watched him from behind her big glasses, which he'd really like to lift off her face so he could better read her expression.

"Not really, but I guess for the next day we don't have a choice. The hotel is sold out and I don't plan to move to another hotel."

She nodded as if she'd already known. Perhaps she'd called the front desk and asked.

Slade had never been an awkward kind of person. Usually, he could come up with something funny to say, something to smooth over any situation. This wasn't any ordinary situation, though. This was him standing in a hotel room with his wife, whom he didn't want to be his wife and neither did she want to be his wife.

He raked his fingers through his hair then, shrugged.

"I'll just grab my suit and change." He opened the closet door and removed a garment bag. "I'll hurry in the bathroom so I won't interfere with you getting ready. If you're going, that is."

"I'm going."

He nodded and turned toward the bathroom.

"With you."

He paused, but didn't turn around. "Why?"

"As far as the world is concerned, we're happy newlyweds. If we go separately, we'll have to answer too many questions. I don't know about you, but I've dealt with enough questions about our marriage already today."

Slade looked up at the ceiling, counted to ten, then turned. "That's my fault. I'm sorry. You're right. I prefer not to raise questions, but even if we're together, people are going to be curious."

"You're right, but at least if we're together we can keep our story straight."

"I won't lie to anyone who asks about us."

"You're going to tell people that you married me so you could have sex with me?"

When she said it out loud, he agreed the reason sounded ridiculous. Still...

"Isn't that why most men get married?" he said, fighting to keep his tone light. "Because they want to have sex with the woman they are marrying? I definitely want to have sex with you, Taylor."

"I suppose so," she responded, ignoring his last comment. "Or we could just tell them that we were drunk and didn't realize what we were doing."

He certainly hadn't been thinking clearly, but he distinctly recalled exchanging vows with her, promising to care for her forever, to cherish her and yet they were planning to end things before they'd even got started.

He stared at her, wishing he could read whatever was running through that sharp mind of hers. "Shall we tell them we married because we were drunk or because we wanted to have sex?"

Her gaze darted about the room as if seeking the answer somewhere within the four walls. Finally, she shrugged. "Take your pick. Both are true."

Taylor pulled her dress out of the closet. Her gaze settled on Slade's clothes hanging next to hers.

Other than her father, she'd never lived with a man, so seeing the mix of Slade's belongings with hers had her pausing, had her eyes watering up again.

What an emotional roller coaster she rode.

Her safe, secure world felt as if it was crumbling around her.

She'd quit taking chances years ago. Had quit living in some ways. Oh, she lived through Gracie, but what about for herself? Nina was right. She didn't do anything for herself, just lived in a nice controlled environment where she planned for all contingencies.

Too bad she hadn't had a backup plan for an unexpected Vegas Christmas wedding.

While Slade was in the bathroom, she changed into her dress, took her hair down from its tight pin-back and pulled it up into a looser hold. She had her contacts in her purse, but wasn't sure what it would say if she put them in when she almost always wore her glasses.

How ridiculous was she being? What did it matter what she looked like?

Still, she dug in her purse and put in her contacts. She

was just blinking them into place when Slade stepped out of the bathroom.

Wearing only his suit pants.

Taylor's body responded to his bare chest like a Pavlov dog to its stimulus. The man was beautiful.

And hers.

Not for long, but at this moment Slade Sain was hers more than any other man had ever been.

Just as she was his more than any other woman had ever been his.

Maybe.

She frowned because she really didn't know that to be true. "Have you been married before?"

Her question obviously caught him off guard. "No. Why? Have you? Never mind, silly question with that one-guy thing. You haven't."

"No, I haven't," she agreed, averting her gaze from his intense blue one. "I just wondered if you had."

Despite the tension between them, he grinned with wry humor. "Wondering if I make marrying a habit?"

Exactly. "Something like that."

He slipped his crisp blue shirt on one arm at a time, then buttoned his cuffs. "I've never been married before." He paused, stared at her with a serious look. "I've never even contemplated marriage."

Her feet wanted to shuffle but she somehow kept them still. "Why not?"

Smoothing out his shirt, he shrugged. "I have other plans for my life besides a wife, two point five kids and a white picket fence."

Her chest spasmed at just how different they really were, because once upon a time she'd dreamed of being a wife with kids and that proverbial white picket fence. "I'm sorry."

"Don't be. We're human and made a mistake. People do it all the time."

He wasn't telling her anything she didn't know. So why

did his words shoot arrows into her chest? "Not me. Not like this." She winced. "I mean, obviously I have made mistakes before, but I thought I'd learned better than to make this kind."

"Marrying me makes you realize you haven't evolved as far as you'd hoped?"

"Something like that. We were practically strangers and got married." Sighing, she closed her eyes. "Before last night you probably didn't even know my eye color."

"I knew."

His answer was so quick, so confident, that she couldn't question the truth of his response.

Staring at him, she asked, "How?"

He shoved his hands in his pants pockets. "I know more about you than you seem to think."

"Like what?"

"Like how much you love coffee."

She rolled her eyes. "Lots of people love coffee, so that's just a generic assumption that could be said about a high percentage of the population."

He shook his head. "You like two teaspoons of cream and one packet of sweetener."

She frowned. That was how she took her coffee. For a moment he had her, but she hadn't made it through medical school by being easily duped. "You saw me make my coffee this morning."

"You're right," he agreed, walking back to the closet to pick up his sleek black dress shoes. "I did. But I already knew how you took your coffee because I make a point to be near the lounge when you go for your morning cup at eight forty-five every day."

That he knew what time she took a coffee break was a little uncanny. Maybe she was more easily duped than she'd realized.

"What else do you know?"

"That you smile a lot at work. That your patients love you. That Mr. Gonzales has a crush on you."

"Mr. Gonzales has a crush on every female who works at the clinic," she pointed out about one of her favorite patients. The older man came in weekly for his lung-cancer treatments and the staff adored him.

"You're his favorite."

"Maybe." She watched Slade sit on the bed and slip on his socks, then his shoes. "What else?"

He lowered his foot back to the carpet but remained seated on the bed. Good. She didn't want him towering over her. "Blue is your favorite color. Not a regular blue, a turquoise blue."

"How would you know that?"

"Because you wear that color more than any other."

He knew what she wore? Why would he have noticed her clothes? Especially since she usually had her lab coat on over whatever she wore?

"You're starting to creep me out a little."

"Surely you noticed that I'd been trying to get to know you for months. I start a conversation and you end it with a few words. I walk up to you and you walk off. I ask you out, you say no."

Of course she'd said no. He wasn't her type.

"You talk to all the women at the clinic," she pointed out.

"I talk to everyone at the clinic. Not just the women."

"True, but you're a horrible flirt."

He looked amused. "I've never made any bones about the fact that I enjoy women but that I have no intentions of settling down. I wanted to take you out, for us to enjoy our time together, and then us both move on to what we really want in life."

Taylor gulped. He sounded so much like Kyle...only Kyle had never been so honest with her, had never told her that he'd been seeing other women, that she hadn't been special. Quite the opposite. He'd made her believe she'd been his one and only.

"I date, Taylor, and I have flirted with women in the past. But for however long it takes for our lawyers to sort out this mess, I will be faithful to you. You have my word on that."

Something in his voice rang of truth, but she couldn't think straight for the heat flushing her face.

"I wasn't… I mean… I haven't slept with a man for over six years so it's a safe bet to say that for however long we're married I'll be faithful to you as well."

From his seat on the bed, he stared at her. "You're a young, beautiful woman, Taylor. Why is it that you've not had sex in six years?"

She gave him a classic "duh" look. "Because I have Gracie."

Obviously, he knew nothing about raising a six-year-old girl, about being a good mother, about trying to live up to her parents' expectations of her to be a responsible woman. Apparently.

"Being a mother doesn't make you less of a woman, Taylor. Or make you have fewer physical needs."

"Being a mother means I have to make responsible decisions because my choices don't just affect me, but her as well." With each word she said, bits of her carefully constructed facade crumbled. "She's not going to understand that I got married while in Vegas."

"Don't tell her."

Taylor bit the inside of her lower lip. He was right. She could just not tell Gracie. She and Slade would divorce and her daughter would never know the difference. Only her daughter really did have big ears. What if Gracie found out and *she* hadn't been the one to tell her?

She didn't begin to fool herself that her parents wouldn't find out. They'd be so disappointed. Again. Not that they didn't love Gracie, but that Taylor had once again not followed their norm would earn another tsk from her mother and another sigh from her father.

"What if Gracie overheard something or someone else told her? That wouldn't be fair to her."

His expression was pinched. "I'm sure you know best."

"Clearly not."

"Or you wouldn't have married me?" His tone held wry humor.

"I'm sure for other women and under different circumstances, a woman marrying you wouldn't be considered a bad thing. But not me."

Sliding his hands into his pants pockets, he frowned. "Why not?"

Seriously? He was asking her why not? The man was the office playboy and she was the quiet mouse.

"You have to admit you aren't exactly daddy material."

Daddy material. Not that Slade wanted to be daddy material, but Taylor's words stung. So, he had absolutely no experience being a father and had no desire to learn. That didn't mean he'd be a bad one. Every guy started somewhere.

For her to judge him so unfairly irked.

"Has it occurred to you that I could already have a child on the way?"

Her face paled to an icky green shade. "We made more than one mistake last night, didn't we?"

Slade's chest threatened to turn inside out. His heart pounded and his throat constricted at the ramifications of what they were discussing. "If you are pregnant, Taylor, I'll take care of you and our child."

Taylor surprised him by sinking onto the bed beside him. "Gracie is the best thing that ever happened to me, but I don't want another kid, Slade. Not like this."

Which meant she did want more kids someday. No doubt she was a wonderful mother. Too bad he didn't want a wife and kids because he couldn't imagine anyone better than Taylor.

He sighed at how different they were tonight with each other compared to the previous night. The night before they'd both been carefree, full of lust and passion for each other.

"I wish we could go back to last night."

"Why?" she whispered from beside him. Why she whispered he wasn't sure, but somehow her low voice seemed exactly right.

"Last night I wasn't your enemy."

Her head fell forward and she stared at her hands, no doubt at the shiny thin band on her left hand. With the way she felt, why was she still wearing the cheap strip of gold?

"You aren't my enemy, Slade."

Her words should have comforted him, but her tone wasn't complimentary.

"You're right," he conceded. "I'm your husband. That's worse."

"I'm sorry." She sounded as if she truly was.

"Tell me, Taylor, would things have been different this morning if we'd had sex without getting married?"

She shrugged. "I don't think I would have had sex without marriage. Not really. After I got pregnant with Gracie, and Kyle signed away his rights, I vowed I wouldn't give myself to another man unless he married me first." She toyed with the gold band on her finger, then stood and walked across the room, turning to look at where he sat. "Foolishly, I equated marriage as being loved truly and completely." She laughed a little, but there wasn't any real humor in the sound. She spread her arms and gave a smile that was more sad than anything else. "Look at me now, desperate for a divorce less than twenty-four hours after getting married. Guess that old saying about being careful what you wish for definitely applies in this case."

Slade couldn't bear the self-condemnation that shone in

her eyes. He crossed the room to stand in front of her. He knew better than to take her in his arms, although that's exactly what he wanted to do. Instead, he traced his finger along her hairline, then cupped her chin. Her eyes, unfettered by her glasses, glittered up at him like big and beautiful emeralds.

Guilt hit him. She wanted exactly the opposite from life. She wanted that white picket fence and two point five kids. Instead, she was married to him.

"I am looking, Taylor. I see a woman who fascinates me, a woman who is strong and good and beautiful. A woman who turns me on and makes my blood boil. We aren't enemies. We made a mistake in getting married, but we're in agreement on ending the marriage. Our mistake is a fixable one." Did he really believe his own words? He wasn't sure. He just didn't want their mistake ruining her life. "I want to spend the evening with you without what happened last night as a barrier between us. Even if just for tonight."

She considered him a few moments, emotions playing across her face. "Just for tonight? Pretend that everything is okay? Why?"

"Why not? What do we have to lose by putting forward a united front? We both want a divorce. We're on the same page. Why suffer through the evening alone when even despite our emotional turmoil the physical is still booming between us?"

She blinked up at him. "It's what Nina said I should do... I want to, Slade, but... Okay."

A flicker of emotion he couldn't label burned to life within him. Crazy because the last thing he needed was to get more entangled with Taylor. A voice in his head reminded him that he was married to her. How much more entangled could one get?

CHAPTER FIVE

Slade was the perfect date. Maybe because he was trying so hard. Taylor knew he was trying and appreciated the effort he was exerting to make her evening as stress-free as possible, especially when she knew he wasn't any happier about their current circumstances than she was.

The meal had been the usual conference menu of a spinach salad, slightly rubbery chicken, green beans and potatoes. For dessert, they'd had a key lime pie that had been quite good.

The final speech of the conference had finished and now the attendees were mingling, with a few heading onto the dance floor and others to the main section of the hotel to gamble.

"You guys want to come with us to the blackjack table?" Dr. Ryan joined the conversation they'd been having with a couple of oncologists from Gainesville, Florida.

Slade's gaze connected with hers and she shook her head.

"Sorry, bud," Slade told his colleague. "But Taylor and I won't be doing any gambling tonight. I was just about to take her out onto the dance floor."

The dance floor? Taylor wanted to protest, but Cole Ryan was watching her reaction a bit too closely so she just smiled.

"Ha, marriage is a gamble every night," Dr. Ryan joked as Slade took Taylor's hand and led her from the group.

"I never knew he had such a sour disposition regarding marriage," Taylor mused, trying to focus on the other man and not on how good it felt for Slade to be holding her hand, on how her heart was racing at his nearness, at how her skin burned at his touch.

"Perhaps it's only your marriage to me that sours his disposition."

Taylor frowned. "You think he…? No, I mean he asked me out once, but that was a long time ago. We just didn't hit it off that way."

"That way?" Slade's face darkened and if Taylor didn't know better she'd think he was jealous. But that made no sense. They had no real ties to each other, only plans to divorce as soon as possible.

"You know, like…" She paused. She'd been going to say like she and Slade had because the biggest problem she'd had with Cole Ryan had been that there had been no sparks. Otherwise he'd been a decent guy who had met most of the criteria on her Mr. Right list.

Slade had the sparks covered and then some. Right now, with her hand in his as he led her onto the dance floor, she knew exactly how they'd ended up where they had the night before. When he touched her, fireworks went off inside her body. Last night he'd had the whole Fourth of July show exploding within her.

She swallowed, willed her body to not give in to its carnal reactions to Slade, to focus on anything but the fire between them.

Dinner had gone well. He'd had intelligent conversations with the other people at their table, had included her, asked her opinions, and sat back and let her give those opinions with admiration in his eyes. He'd been attentive, pulling out her chair, touching her frequently, smiling at her often. When an overly pompous member of their table had gone on and on about the latest article he'd written about the denucleation of a cloned T-cell, they'd shared a look that had spoken volumes without saying a word, because they'd known what the other had been thinking. His wink had reached inside her and touched something tender.

If she hadn't known he was Dr. Slade Sain, playboy extraordinaire, if she hadn't made the mistake of marrying him, she might think he was someone she would like to date. Which was kind of silly since she was already married to him. And he *was* Dr. Slade Sain, playboy extraordinaire.

He'd said he'd be faithful for however long they were married. An easy promise since they planned to talk to divorce attorneys as soon as they returned home. Still, tonight, at this moment, it was easy to pretend that their attraction was special, that the future was full of wonderful possibilities.

What was it Nina had said? To let loose and enjoy herself? That she was married to a hunk so why not enjoy it for the rest of their Vegas stay? To worry about tomorrow… tomorrow.

Slade pulled her into his arms and, her arms around him, she buried her face into the curve of his neck. He smelled so good. So perfectly male.

He was perfectly male. His body. His mind. His sense of humor.

She wanted to cry. She wanted to forget who she was and who she had to be. She wanted to be that woman Nina had told her to be, even if only until she had to fly home tomorrow evening.

Slade drew back and looked down at her. "You okay?"

She nodded and toyed with where his hair brushed the back of his collar. "This pretend stuff isn't so bad."

One corner of his mouth lifted. "Agreed. You are very beautiful, Taylor. No pretending."

Her breath caught because he looked at her as if she were the most beautiful woman he'd ever seen. How could he look at her that way? As if she was the only woman who existed?

"Thank you. You aren't bad yourself." She attempted to lighten the heavy longing clouding her good intentions.

"If you could read my mind, you'd think every thought in my head was bad."

"Oh?"

He shook his head.

"You can't say something like that and then not tell me what you were thinking."

"Says who?"

"Me."

His lips twitched. "I'm thinking that perhaps holding you in my arms in public wasn't such a good idea, because having you pressed against my body makes me respond in a very nonpublic way."

"I noticed that."

"Kinda hard to miss."

"Did you say hard?"

His mouth was close to hers. So very close. "Isn't this about the point in our conversation where we got into trouble last night?"

"The point where we started being suggestive?" she whispered against his lips. For twenty-four hours she could let go and just be a woman who was with a man who turned her on, a woman who was with a man who wanted her.

"The point where I wanted you so badly I couldn't think of anything else but having you."

"There's only one problem." She stared into his eyes, seeing passion and something so intense it stole her breath. For twenty-four hours he was hers. Twenty-four hours and what they did wouldn't change anything. Twenty-four hours and then they'd return to reality.

"What's that?"

"I won't sleep with anyone who isn't my husband."

"And your husband?" he breathed against her lips. "You'll sleep with him?"

"Sleep? If you think we will be sleeping anytime soon, then you aren't nearly as turned on as I am."

He kissed her. Right there on the dance floor his mouth covered hers for a gentle kiss that was so potent it demanded everything she had yet gave so much more.

When he pulled back, he leaned his forehead against hers. "If we do this, nothing changes between us. We'll still end this as soon as possible. You know that, right?"

Taylor was pretty sure all that could change between them already had. They couldn't ever go back to the way things had been. With the way he was looking at her, she didn't want to. Tomorrow night they'd be back in Tennessee, reality would take over and they'd never have this moment again.

Nothing would ever be the same and if she thought about it that would terrify her.

So, instead, she clasped her hands with his and told him with her eyes what she wanted.

The night before they'd been frantic for each other.

Now, back in their hotel room, Taylor felt just as frantic, but was enjoying Slade's slow stripping of her way too much to urge him to go faster.

She wavered between eyes closed in ecstasy and open to view the fantasy of his caresses. She watched him in the dresser mirror. He stood behind her, his hand on her dress, his other at her waist as he slowly slid her zipper down her back. His mouth trailed kisses in the wake of exposed skin, causing goose bumps along her spine that scattered outward in pleasured awareness of his gentle caress.

He reached the curve of her spine and slid his hands beneath the silky material. "You aren't wearing a bra."

"There was no need. The dress has built-in support."

"Lucky dress to be next to these." His hands were now on her bare breasts, covering them, cupping them as he straightened to kiss her shoulder. His gaze met hers in the mirror as his lips spread more kisses along her nape. "Very lucky dress, but it's got to go."

He maneuvered the material to where it fell to her waist, then slipped the dress over her hips to leave her standing in her black lace panties.

His body pressed against her from behind, he examined her reflection. "You are so beautiful, Taylor."

"Don't look too close or you'll see my many flaws," she half teased, self-conscious of the changes pregnancy had left on her body. She didn't have a lot of stretch marks, true, but she did have them.

Slade spun her, knelt in front of her and brushed his lips over the small silvery streaks that marred her abdomen near her right hip.

"You are beautiful. All of you," he praised, his lips moving to her left side and kissing the tiny silver lines there.

Taylor shuddered, her hands going to his shoulders as her knees threatened to buckle.

Weak as water. She'd heard the expression used in the past but had never really understood the term until this moment. Her legs were weak as water, threatening to let her spill to the floor in a gooey gush.

His tongue traced over her belly, darting into her belly button. His hands molded her to him, helping to support her.

He moved higher up her belly, causing her breath to suck in as his face brushed against her breasts.

She closed her eyes and just felt. She felt every touch, every caress, every move of his body against hers.

She felt every emotion, every ounce of passion, every demand for more.

When she could stand no more of his sweet, torturous foreplay, she tugged on his shoulders. "Please, Slade. Please!"

He stood, took her mouth with his, and kissed her so hard that she thought they might always stay that way, that their locked lips knew something far beyond what their minds did, that they belonged together.

Not breaking their kiss, he lifted her. She wrapped her legs around his waist, not liking that his pants were in the way, not liking that he was still so dressed when she was so naked.

When he lowered her onto their bed, breaking their kiss, she immediately tugged his shirt free from his waistband. "I want to touch you."

"Good." His breathing was heavy. "I want you to touch me."

"I mean now. Before. I want to touch you the way you touched me."

His hands stilled from where he'd been unbuttoning his shirt. "I'm all yours."

Taylor sneaked a peek at the man sitting in the airplane seat next to her. He'd offered the guy who had originally had the seat a hundred dollars to swap and the guy had traded without hesitation. Currently, Slade's nose was buried in the program he was reading on his computer tablet.

"Quit looking at me like that."

"Sorry." Heat flushed her face. "Like what?"

"Like you are trying to dissect me."

"Sorry. That wasn't my intention."

Slade clicked a button on the tablet, closing the program he'd been reading, then turned to her. "What was your intention?"

"Pardon?"

"Why were you looking at me just then?"

"I...I don't know."

"Yes, you do. Tell me."

"That's ridiculous."

"You were thinking about this weekend, about all the things that happened between us, and you were wonder-

ing about what's going to happen once this plane lands,"
he supplied for her.

"You're wrong."

His brow arched.

"At least, partially. I was thinking about this weekend
and what happened between us, but I already know what's
going to happen once this plane lands."

He waited.

"Nina and my daughter will be waiting to pick me up.
I'll go home with them. You and I will get divorced and will
forget this weekend ever happened."

He digested her words for a few minutes, seeming to accept her prediction. His lips thinned to a straight line. "Except for the whole getting-married thing, I don't regret this
weekend, Taylor."

Her heart fluttered at his words, but she tried not to read
too much into his comment. Did she regret the weekend?
The past twenty-four hours had been amazing. Waking up
in his arms and making love first thing this morning, then
again in the shower before they'd checked out of the hotel
had been amazing. Dealing with the ramifications of what
they'd done at the North Pole Christmas Bliss Wedding
Chapel was what wasn't so amazing.

She tried not to touch her ring. She failed.

"We were in Vegas. People do silly things in Vegas. We'll
be home soon and the best thing we can do is forget any of
this ever happened," she whispered, even though she seriously doubted any of the surrounding passengers could hear
their conversation.

"I basically agree. A wife and kid aren't on my agenda,
but I'll admit—" he gave her a sexy grin "—you're going
to be hard to forget."

Not nearly as hard as it was going to be to forget him.

"Maybe we could still see each other occasionally," he
suggested.

Oh, how he tempted her. But to delay the inevitable would only complicate an already bad situation even further.

"We had a fun little fling this weekend, but when this plane lands everything goes back to normal. I'm a single mother with a very busy schedule. I just don't have the time or inclination for an affair with you."

"We're not exactly having an affair," he pointed out. "We're married."

"A marriage we both want ended as soon as possible. Santa Claus married us in a building that looked like a life-sized gingerbread house. Elves sold us our rings, took our picture, witnessed the ceremony. Who knows if our certificate is even real? It's probably not since it was issued after normal business hours."

Guilt hit her. She sounded crude and uncaring. But, really, what did he expect? They didn't even know each other. Not beyond the physical. That she knew quite well. She'd saved every pore on his body to memory because she'd known she'd want to pull out the memories and relive them.

"It's something to have our lawyers look into. If it's not real that would certainly simplify things.

"I don't get that lucky," she mused, thinking how great it would be if their wedding turned out to not be a legally binding union.

He took her hand into his. "You're right. Our wedding ceremony being a sham would be in both of our best interests."

She'd just said the same thing. So why did hearing him say the words cut into her chest? Make her want to hold on to his hand all the tighter?

She might have only spent two nights in his arms, but part of her felt he was hers. No doubt her feelings were just associations to the phenomenal sex they'd had. Women had been associating great sex with emotions for centuries. He'd done great things to her body in bed and out of bed. Of course she'd feel possessive of him.

What was she thinking? She wasn't thinking, that was the problem. That had been the problem all weekend.

"Physically, I still want you, Taylor. I'd like to see you again."

Physically, she still wanted him, too, but she couldn't afford an affair with Slade. "I've more to think about than just myself."

"Your daughter?"

"Yes. Gracie is my whole world. I won't expose her to this mess I've created."

"I'm really not interested in meeting your daughter or becoming a part of your day-to-day life."

"Just in meeting up with me for sex?"

"I guess that makes me sound like a jerk," he admitted, and she wasn't going to argue with him. He sounded exactly as she'd known all along.

"It doesn't make you sound like someone I want to invest more time in."

"I guess I understand that, considering you do have a kid." The look on his face said he didn't really. Or maybe it was just the prospect of her being a mother that caused the look of disgust. "I'm being selfish in that I want you in my life still."

"Just without the entanglements of marriage and my daughter?"

His grin was self-deprecating. "There I go sounding like a jerk again."

"I'll contact a lawyer and we'll divorce quietly. We both know it was a mistake, that we can chalk this weekend up to a great sexual adventure, and we can go about undoing our mistake in a completely civil way."

He studied her a moment, then nodded. "I guess you're right. I just…"

"You just what?"

"I enjoyed our time together."

His words struck deep inside her.

"That makes two of us," she admitted. She'd had such high hopes that someday she would find the right man, would marry and have a happy little family. The house, white picket fence, children, happiness.

"Seems a little sad when we are so physically compatible," Slade interrupted her thoughts.

"Perhaps." A lot sad, really. "But better we be logical and end this now than risk things getting messier."

He took her hand into his, laced their fingers and traced over her skin with his thumb. "Things would only get messier if we let them. As long as we knew the score, that we weren't long term, we could give each other great pleasure."

Taylor sighed. If Gracie hadn't been involved, she might give in to the temptation deep within her. But her daughter was involved. Gracie needed stability. Not a mother who ran out and got married in Vegas to the office playboy, planned to divorce him but wanted to keep having sex with him until the divorce was final. Slade made her act out of character, made her behave rashly. She owed it to Gracie, to her daughter's future and well-being, to make responsible choices.

Having an affair with Slade wouldn't be responsible.

"Therein lies the problem. I don't want to continue this in hopes it wouldn't get messier." When he started to interrupt her, she rushed on. "Admittedly, it would be a pleasurable mistake but a mistake all the same. We were in Vegas and got caught up in the silliness. Let's end things now while we can still be civil to each other and this, hopefully, won't ruin our ability to work in the same clinic together. I really like my job and don't want to have to look for something else."

"Mommy!" Arms spread wide, a pint-size fairy princess ran toward Taylor. "I missed you."

The moment she was off the escalator that led down to the airport's baggage area Taylor knelt down to her daughter's level and scooped her into her arms. She kissed the top of Gracie's head, breathing in the fresh baby-shampoo scent of her blond curls. "I missed you, too!"

"You shouldn't go away for so long ever again," Gracie scolded.

"It was only three nights."

"That's too long."

Three nights in which a lifetime of changes had taken place because as much as she told herself she would put the weekend's events behind her, it wouldn't be that simple. If only.

She hugged Gracie tightly. "You're right. That was way too long to be away from my best girl."

"I'm your only girl," Gracie reminded her with a giggle. "Aunt Nina and I put up her Christmas tree and she let me hang the ornaments and a stocking with my name on it. Do you think Santa will leave my presents at Aunt Nina's house?"

"Maybe Santa will leave you a present at Aunt Nina's, too, but Santa knows where to leave your presents." Taylor squeezed her daughter and kissed the top of her head again. Emotion clogged her throat at how much this talkative little girl meant to her. "That's some outfit you have going there."

Taylor raised her gaze to Nina.

"What can I say?" Nina smiled and shrugged. "She wanted to be a fairy princess. Who am I to deny her inner princess?"

"I am a fairy princess," Gracie corrected Taylor's best friend and nurse, then redirected her attention to her mother. "Aunt Nina wouldn't wear her princess clothes because she thought she might get 'rested, but I think mine are beautiful." Gracie spun as if to prove her point, curtsied, then snuggled back to where her mother still crouched down.

"Oh?" Taylor arched a brow at her friend, smothering a laugh at the mental image of Nina wearing a fairy-princess outfit in the Nashville airport.

"I figured someone would call airport security if I came

in dressed like a cartoon princess," Nina admitted, gesturing to her jeans. "I tried to convince Gracie I was a princess in disguise, but she wasn't buying it."

"Princesses don't wear jeans when they're in disguise," Gracie reported matter-of-factly, her fingers going to Taylor's hair and twining beneath the pulled-back strands. Playing with Taylor's hair was something Gracie had started as a baby while nursing and something she reverted to almost always if she was in Taylor's lap or snuggled up next to her. Taylor treasured the bond with her daughter and dropped another kiss to her forehead.

"Did you bring me a present from Vegas?"

Taylor's stomach plummeted. Gracie's present. How could she have forgotten Gracie's present? She'd even mentioned to Slade this morning that she needed to stop by one of the hotel's many gift shops and pick out something special for her daughter. Instead, she'd gotten wet and wild with him in the shower and completely forgotten.

She stared into her daughter's wide expectant green eyes. Oh, yeah, she'd been irresponsible this weekend, had been a big disappointment to her child and would be mailing off her application for Worst Mom in the History of the World later this week. Yet another reason why ending things with Slade was the right decision. He made her forget things she'd never have forgotten otherwise. "I—"

"I think this is for you."

Taylor almost toppled over at the sound of Slade's voice. They'd purposely parted at the gate. He hadn't wanted to meet Gracie any more than she'd wanted him to. He'd leaned in, kissed her cheek and told her he'd had a great time, minus the whole wedding thing. She'd laughed, nodded and ducked into the bathroom to hide the moisture that had stung her eyes.

Still in a kneeling position, she glanced up at where he stood, his overnight bag draped across his shoulder, his clothes impeccable, not looking at all as if he'd been on a plane for several hours. He held a fuzzy stuffed bear wearing a pink tutu and a glitzy pink crown on her head.

Where had he gotten that? One of the Nashville airport gift shops? Had to be. He'd been at her side at the Vegas airport.

His face was pale and yet had pink splotches on his cheeks as he stared at her daughter. He eyed her as if she might morph into a monster and devour him any moment.

Gracie, never one to be too shy, spotted the bear and grinned with excitement. "I think you're right."

Her tone sounded so mature, so confident that had it not been Slade holding the bear, had he not been looking in such a shell-shocked and leery way at the little girl, Taylor would have laughed at her daughter's expression and words. Instead, all she could think was that she wanted to grab Gracie and run far away from him.

Which made no sense.

She didn't need to protect her daughter from Slade. Yet that's exactly the instinct that rose to the surface. Not that there was any need. He looked ready to bolt at any second. He should have stayed away.

"Hello, Dr. Sain," Nina greeted him, looking quite intrigued. "I hear congratulations are in order."

Taylor wanted to kick her friend, but had to settle for a warning look. Gracie's fingers left her hair and moved to hold Taylor's hand as she eagerly eyed the bear.

"Thanks," he answered, some color coming back to his face. Regaining his composure, he flashed a smile that would weaken many a female knee.

Good thing Taylor was already kneeling down because her knees wobbled.

Gracie felt her shift and frowned at her. "Mommy, are you okay?"

Not really, but she couldn't tell her daughter that because Gracie would want to know what was wrong. What could she say? That she'd spent the past two days having wild Vegas sex with this man, her husband, but now she just wanted to go back to her ordinary life and forget anything out of the ordinary had happened?

Was that what she wanted? What she really wanted? Or did she want something more? Something that made no logical sense whatsoever? Something he'd never give her and so she didn't dare even think it? If she'd had the slightest doubt, seeing his reaction to Gracie would have reconfirmed that he wasn't right for them.

"Mommy is fine, Princess Gracie." This came from Nina, who apparently took pity on Taylor's inability to talk. "She's just had a long flight home from Vegas and is a little tired."

When no one made a move, Gracie gestured toward the bear that an also silent Slade still held. "Did my mommy bring that for my present?"

Perhaps she wasn't the only one struck speechless because, despite the smile he'd flashed, Slade just stared at Gracie as if he'd never seen a kid before, then tentatively held out the bear to her.

First getting a nod from Taylor, Gracie took the bear and cuddled it. "Thank you. I love her. I'm going to call her Vegas, Princess Vegas, because she came all the way in an airplane to live with me."

Slade opened his mouth, probably to tell Gracie the truth, that he'd bought the bear in a Nashville gift shop, but Nina stopped him.

"Gracie, that's a really cool name for a really cool bear. Can I see her?"

Gracie hugged the bear, but then showed it to Nina, pointing out a tiny pink bejeweled necklace on the toy.

"Thank you." Taylor finally found words as she straightened.

His gaze shifted to Gracie.

Taylor cast a nervous glance toward her daughter, who was still busy checking out the bear with Nina. Her friend was trying to look as if she wasn't paying attention to Taylor and Slade, but was, no doubt, soaking up every word.

His expression was serious. His blue eyes dark and intense. "I felt responsible for you not having her gift."

Taylor swallowed. "It's my fault, not yours. I let myself get distracted."

"I'm sorry, Taylor." His gaze held hers, then shifted back to Gracie. "So sorry."

"Mommy, can we go home now?" Gracie interrupted, tugging on Taylor's hand. "I want to show you the picture Aunt Nina helped me paint and we need to find a Christmas tree. Aunt Nina's is so beautiful."

Nina shot her an apologetic look at not being able to keep Gracie distracted longer.

Taylor didn't care. She didn't want to be having this conversation with Slade.

"I'm sorry, too." Taylor spotted her suitcase rolling out on the nearby baggage carousel. "Now, if you'll excuse me, I'm going to grab my bag and go home to catch up with my daughter. Goodbye."

Just before it got too far for her to catch this time around, Taylor pulled her bag off the rolling contraption. She smiled at Nina and Gracie, and pretended everything was great. "Let's go. Not sure I'm up to going out to buy a Christmas tree tonight, but I can't wait to get home and see that picture."

First waving goodbye to a stiff Slade and thanking him again for her bear, Gracie slipped her hand into Taylor's and began talking a mile a minute, as she usually did.

Too bad Taylor wasn't able to keep from looking back when they reached the glass doors to take them out of the airport.

Slade still stood right where they'd left him.

CHAPTER SIX

SLADE LOOKED OVER his patient's labs. Her white blood cell count was too low to administer her chemotherapy.

"We'll recheck your levels next week and administer then if you're strong enough to handle the treatment."

The pale woman nodded. Twenty-three years old and fighting leukemia with all she had, Brittany Tremaine hadn't lost her hair yet, but was experiencing other devastating side effects of her therapy. "Whatever you say, Doc."

The young man beside her, holding her hand, leaned forward. "What do we do in the meantime?"

"In the meantime, she needs to rest, eat healthily, build her strength back up." Slade stood, shook the man's hand, then gave Brittany a hug that he hoped conveyed encouragement and compassion. It was what he felt for the young woman, what he felt for so many of his patients.

Oncology wasn't a profession for the faint of heart.

When his mother had died of breast cancer when he'd been twelve, Slade had become obsessed with fighting cancer. He'd held fundraisers at his school, become an advocate at raising awareness of the deadly disease, had known that he'd go into a profession where he could continue that battle and make a difference to where other kids didn't have to face the same thing he had.

Although there was a great emotional burden that came along with his job, there was also a great deal of joy and satisfaction with each success story. He prayed Brittany would be one of those success stories.

"I'll see you around the same time next week. If anything changes negatively before then, come back in sooner," he advised, tearing off a piece of paper from a preprinted pad he kept in his pocket. A motivational quote was on the sticky note.

Slade gave a quote to each and every patient he saw each and every time he saw them. Perhaps a silly habit, but he'd had several patients comment on his messages, that they'd kept them posted on their mirrors. One survivor told him she'd kept the quotes in a scrapbook and now shared the book with others when the need arose.

Slade knew all too well about saving quotes. He had a stack of them himself. He'd not looked at them in several years, but last night, when he'd gotten home from Vegas and unpacked his suitcase, he'd pulled the shoebox he kept the notes in out from his closet. He'd flipped through the protective album he'd placed them in years ago as a young boy, and he read each and every one. Right up until the shaky handwriting had become almost illegible.

Then he'd called his dad.

When he'd gone to bed he'd been an emotional wreck in some ways, but in others he'd known exactly what he had to do. Although he couldn't stay married to Taylor, he didn't want to hurt his family, or hers. Most importantly, he didn't want to hurt Taylor.

The best way to achieve all of that was for them to pretend they were happily married, then, when he hopefully got the job with Grandview, he could leave as the bad guy, and she'd not suffer any negativity from their impromptu wedding. Should he tell her about his interview? Perhaps, but at this point, he suspected she'd use the fact that he might be leaving to be that much more on guard with him. Taylor already aced on guard so he'd just wait and tell her if the need arose.

"Dr. Sain?" Nina interrupted his thoughts. "Sorry to bother you, but Taylor is in a room with a patient and I need someone to check a patient now, please. I believe she's having a reaction to her infusion medication."

Slade shoved his nostalgia down and followed Taylor's nurse to where a woman who appeared to be in her early fifties sat in one of the special recliners in the infusion lounge.

"Hello, Mrs. Jamison. My name is Dr. Sain. Your nurse tells me you aren't feeling well?"

"I'm itching all over." The woman scratched her neck to prove her point.

Slade skimmed his fingers over her exposed skin. Large red welts were forming. He turned to Nina. "Go ahead and stop her infusion. As long as she isn't allergic to the medications, give her an antihistamine and a shot of steroid."

"Yes, Dr. Sain."

He turned back to the patient. "Any difficulty breathing?"

The woman shook her head. "No, I just itch like crazy and feel a little light-headed."

He examined the woman thoroughly, waited for Nina to administer the medications he'd ordered. "Recheck all her vitals in fifteen minutes and pull me out of a room if you need to."

Nina nodded. "I'll let Taylor know what's going on with her as soon as she's out of her patient room."

As if she'd known they were discussing her, Taylor walked over to them. "Hi, sweetie. Tell me what's happening."

Mrs. Jamison began telling her about how she'd started itching during her infusion.

"Hmm, this is the second time you've received this particular medication. I don't recall any problems with the last infusion. Were there any after you got home?"

Scratching, the woman shook her head. "I felt fine, but I don't now." She cleared her throat. "I feel like my skin is on fire."

Although Slade had just checked the woman, Taylor began examining her. "Heart rate is tachy."

"I gave her an antihistamine and a steroid," Slade informed Taylor. "Hopefully the symptoms will start resolving soon."

The woman hacked then cleared her throat again. "I hope so," she rasped.

"Me, too," Taylor agreed, eyeing the coughing patient with concern. "I think we're going to have to give you another shot of steroid."

"Or maybe just go to epinephrine?" Slade suggested as the woman hacked again. "I think her lips are swelling."

Mrs. Jamison's gaze lifted to them. Her lips were swelling before their eyes. Her eyes watered. Her skin became more and more blotchy. "I feel like I can't get enough air."

"Nina," Taylor said, knowing her nurse would know exactly what she wanted.

"On it," Nina replied, rushing away from them.

"Respiratory rate is over twenty," Taylor said, although Slade wasn't sure if she was speaking to him or was just thinking aloud.

"Take slow deep breaths," Slade advised, in hopes of refocusing the woman's increasing panic. He grasped her wrist and took her pulse. Running over one hundred and fifty, her heart rate was also too high.

"I...can't," the woman denied, shaking her head while coughing. She was now wheezing audibly.

Nina rushed back with an injectable pen that she handed to Taylor. Taylor popped the cap and jabbed the pen down on the woman's thigh, through her clothes, administering the medication in the process.

Slade pulled out his phone and dialed for emergency services.

"I can't...breathe."

"The reaction should be slowing very soon with the medication we just gave," Taylor informed her patient, watching as Slade checked her pulse again. No doubt the adrenaline they'd just administered would push the lady's heart rate up even higher. No matter. There hadn't been a choice. She was going into anaphylactic shock. "You're having an allergic reaction to the chemotherapy medication. It's rare for that to happen but, unfortunately, from time to time it does occur. I'm giving more steroids through your IV and I'm going to admit you to the hospital for observation tonight."

The woman just nodded between wheezes.

"Your heart probably feels as if it's racing like crazy. It is. Although the medicine I just gave can cause an increased heart rate, what I expect to happen is that once your allergic reaction is under control, your heart rate will drop back close to normal."

Taylor and Slade stayed with Mrs. Jamison, keeping her calm and stable while they waited for the ambulance to arrive. Slade soothed the lady in the chair closest to Mrs. Jamison, easing her concerns regarding her own infusion.

"As Taylor said, it's very rare that someone has a reaction to their chemotherapy, but it does happen," he assured the anxious woman, when she asked for her treatment to be stopped for fear she might also react. "You still need your medication infused. Other than prayers, the medication is the best weapon we have at our disposal to fight your cancer."

The nervous woman kept eyeing Mrs. Jamison, but did nod agreement. For a moment Slade had thought she was going to rip out her central line.

Having most of their patients' infusions occur in a common lounge area with recliners and televisions was a good thing overall. It provided support and socialization during the long infusion process. But when something went wrong it could start mayhem.

Fortunately, although the other patients had kept a curious eye on what was happening, only the lady next to Mrs. Jamison seemed spooked.

The paramedics arrived, wheeling in a stretcher.

Taylor gave them a quick report while they loaded a still wheezing and hacking Mrs. Jamison onto the stretcher.

"That scares me," the nervous woman told Slade. "What if I react to my chemo, too?"

"I don't think that's going to happen, Mrs. Smith," he reassured the woman, squeezing her hand gently. "I know putting medications into your body is scary, but there are times when not doing so would be much scarier."

"The medications make me feel so bad," the woman admitted, a little weepy. "Sometimes I feel as if I would be better off to just not take them."

"Your last scans showed a reduction in the size of your tumor. The medications are doing their job. You're doing fantastically on the medicines. To stop them halfway through would be a shame."

Taylor had stayed with her patient until they loaded her onto the ambulance. When she came back into the lounge, she came over to them.

She smiled at Mrs. Smith then glanced at Slade. "Thank you for taking care of Mrs. Jamison."

"You're welcome, but you did all the work."

"I'm not sure why Nina didn't come and get me to begin with. Mrs. Jamison was my patient."

"I had just finished with a patient and was in the hallway. It would have been silly to pull you from an examination room when I was available."

"I suppose you are right." She looked pensive, as if even though she couldn't argue with his logic she didn't really want to agree with him. "Still, I hate it that you had to take care of one of my patients."

Who did she think she was fooling? What she was really saying was that she hated that they'd had to interact. She'd avoided him all morning, including skipping her morning coffee. What was she trying to prove? It wasn't as if the entire office didn't know they'd married and was watching their every move with great curiosity. Such juicy gossip spread like wildfire and, no doubt, the entire clinic had known within an hour of Slade making his announcement during their presentation. If only he'd kept his mouth shut. If only they hadn't gotten married to begin with. If only his chest didn't feel a little like he couldn't breathe when he looked at her. Not that she was looking back. Her eyes were everywhere except meeting his gaze.

"It wasn't a big deal," he said finally, mixed emotions running rampant through him. He wanted her. But that wasn't part of the plan.

"All the same, thank you."

Taylor stared at Slade, feeling as if she should say something more, but what?

What could she possibly say to him? So much and yet, really, what was there to say?

"I had a no-show this morning—she's at home, sick. Can I help you get caught up again?" he offered, taking the pressure off her to come up with something to say.

She shook her head. "That isn't necessary, but thank you."

"I didn't think it was necessary. I just wanted to help you."

"I appreciate the offer, but I don't need your help."

Mrs. Smith was watching their interplay with curious eyes, all concern over her infusion apparently forgotten with the minidrama unfolding in front of her. No doubt the other staff members within viewing distance were also curious bystanders. She'd gotten several congratulations throughout the morning. No doubt Slade had as well.

She'd avoided him. Something she'd gotten good at long ago. Why had Nina gone to him? They'd all worked together for over a year. There were dozens of physicians at the clinic. Never before had Nina had any reason to seek out Slade. Go and marry the man, and suddenly her nurse was asking him to see her patients. Not okay.

Taylor didn't want him seeing her patients. Not when they were having allergic reactions. Not when he'd had a no-show and offered to help her catch up.

Not that she didn't trust him in that regard. He was an excellent doctor. She'd never heard any complaints or problems regarding the care he provided his patients. Quite the opposite. Everyone sang his praises. It was just that the less she had to do with him the better. He wasn't the man for her.

"I'll talk to Nina about not bothering you regarding my patients in the future."

His brow lifted. "Why? We all help each other when the need arises. That's always been the case in this clinic."

Out of respect for the curious ears listening to their conversation and because she didn't want their patients privy to their weekend activities, Taylor just smiled. "You're right. Thank you."

Not that she wouldn't be talking to Nina. She would definitely see to it that Nina went to anyone but Slade for assistance unless a patient's health would otherwise be compromised.

As if he could read her mind, Slade just stared at her. Disappointment showed in his blue eyes. Then he turned to Mrs. Smith. "I'm going to pop in and see whoever is next, but I want to be sure you're okay before I do so. You need anything?"

Taylor didn't wait to hear the woman's response. Slade had the situation under control and the nurses were providing good care for all the other infusion patients. She was going to catch up on her morning patients.

"Do you have a minute?"

Taylor glanced up at the man standing in her doorway. Her husband.

Ugh. Could she lie and say no?

She'd managed to avoid him for the rest of the day, but

had caught him watching her several times when she'd been talking to this patient or that in the infusion lounge.

The last thing she wanted was to spend time with him. Not even a minute. She just wanted to forget he existed, that she had a marriage to do away with, that she had made such a mess of her life over the weekend, that horrific sadness gripped her chest each time she thought of him.

She glanced at Gracie's photo, her greatest happiness in a gray world, and summoned up the courage to meet Slade's gaze.

"What's up?" she asked, pushing her glasses up the bridge of her nose.

He came into her office and shut the door behind him. "We need to talk."

"Not again."

"Did you call a lawyer today?"

"I did." She'd called during the lunch she'd practically inhaled while sitting at her desk. "I have an appointment to meet with her on Friday morning. Did you?"

His lips thinned. "Yes. Oddly enough, I have a Friday morning appointment as well."

Although she hadn't invited him to, he sat down in the seat on the other side of her desk and studied the photo she'd just been looking at. He sat in silence so long, Taylor cleared her throat to remind him she was in the room.

His skin drawn tightly over his cheekbones, he glanced up. "She's a beautiful little girl."

"Thank you."

His gaze drifted back to the photo. "She looks just like you."

"I am her mother." What was he doing?

"What about her father?"

Enough was enough. "Really? You want to discuss Kyle again? Because I don't."

"Does he see Gracie?" Slade persisted.

She eyed him with what had to be pure venom flowing through her veins. Really, that's what the caustic substance sloshing around inside her felt like. Venom. "He doesn't want anything to do with Gracie. He signed away all rights to her."

"Foolish man."

True. As far as Taylor was concerned Kyle had been an idiot to give up his rights to their precious daughter.

"Selfish as this may sound, I'm glad he doesn't want anything to do with her, because I don't believe he'd be a good influence or father. I'd worry about her if she had to spend time in his care and it just makes life simpler that she doesn't have to go back and forth between two houses. As much as I wish he could have been a good father to her, that's not who he is. Gracie has a lot more stability this way."

Slade's gaze met hers. "If Gracie were my daughter, I would spend time with her."

Despite the fact that he'd said he didn't want a wife or kids, he sounded so definite, she didn't doubt his claim. Irrational fear gurgled in her stomach. "Then it's a good thing she's not yours, because I'd worry about her if she was in your care, too."

She didn't add that she worried about Gracie no matter who was watching her. She supposed it was a mother thing, but she wanted to protect her daughter from all the bad things in the world. Leaving her with anyone was difficult. Even leaving her with Nina for the long weekend had been rough, and she trusted her best friend implicitly.

Slade leaned back in the chair and watched her a moment before asking, "Despite how we were this weekend, you don't like me much, do you?"

"Not really."

"Why not?"

"You're not the kind of man I prefer to spend time with."

"Yet you married me."

A vicious throb pounded at her temples. "Don't remind me."

"Why?"

She rubbed her temple, hoping to ease the pulsating pain that she'd begun to associate with thoughts of him. "Why what?"

"Why did you marry me, Taylor?"

She grimaced. "Haven't we already had this conversation?"

"Tell me again."

"I wasn't in my right mind," she said flippantly, wishing she hadn't stayed to do her charting, but had rushed straight out the door as soon as she'd finished with her last patient.

"I haven't been in my right mind since I kissed you in the backseat of that limousine."

His comment surprised Taylor and she met his intent blue gaze. "How so?"

"We're filing for divorce, which is the right thing. I don't want to get entangled in your life, yet I can't stay away from you. I can't go ten minutes without thinking about you." His gaze dropped to the photo of Gracie again, and he winced. "There are a million reasons why I shouldn't, why I should stay away from you and just do as we decided on the plane, but I can't get past the simple fact that I want you, Taylor."

CHAPTER SEVEN

I WANT YOU. Three little words and Slade had Taylor's lungs shriveling up to oxygen-deprived uselessness.

"We don't always get what we want in life, Slade."

Not that she was complaining about her life, but she certainly hadn't.

"Besides, you just want what you can't have."

He shrugged. "We both know that if I kissed you right now, you'd kiss me back."

"I don't know that."

His brow arched. "You think I'm wrong?"

"I think you're wrong," she insisted. In theory, her claim sounded good, but she wasn't so sure he wasn't right. The man's mouth held some kind of power over her.

"Prove it."

Why was she staring at his mouth? Why were his words—"I want you"—echoing through her mind over and over and causing all sorts of jittery reactions inside her body? Want wasn't their problem. They'd wanted each other this past weekend just fine. It was everything else that had been the problem.

"W-what?" she stammered out.

"Prove that my kisses don't affect you." Was it just her or did he look inordinately confident, perhaps even a little arrogant?

"How would I prove that?" Not that she didn't immediately realize the trap he'd set. Darn him. Darn her body's reaction to him.

"Kiss me."

She crossed her arms, realized she probably looked ridiculous and dropped her hands into her lap. "I don't want to kiss you."

"Chicken."

"I'm not going to respond to such a childish taunt."

"Because you know that I'm right." His lips twitched. Oh, yeah, he'd gone from perturbed to haughty.

"You aren't right."

"Unless you prove otherwise, I am right."

Ooh, she really didn't like him.

"Fine, kiss me. But don't be offended when I go rinse my mouth out with peroxide afterwards."

He frowned but moved around the desk, took her hand and pulled her to her feet and into his arms.

The moment her body came into contact with his, she knew she was in trouble. Big trouble.

How could she have forgotten how hard his body was? How good he smelled? How could he even smell that good after working all day? But he did. His spicy male scent teased her nostrils with memories, with acknowledgment that she wanted him.

She expected him to immediately take her mouth, had braced herself for it. Instead, he slipped his fingers around her neck, slowly raking over the sensitive flesh, then pinching her hair clip and releasing her hair.

His fingers threaded into the locks, massaging the base of her scalp, every touch seducing her toward relaxation.

Just get it over with, she wanted to scream.

Or maybe it was just, *Kiss me!* she wanted to shout at him.

Either way, he was taking his dear sweet time and she was growing more and more impatient.

"I said you could kiss me, not maul me."

His eyes sparked with something akin to fire, but he didn't respond except to continue his caress of her and to lower his head.

His lips kissed the corner of her mouth. A soft, brief touch. Then he kissed the other corner.

She fought turning her mouth toward him and somehow managed to stand superstill, as if she was totally unaffected. As if she'd been telling the truth, that his kisses didn't affect her.

But he wasn't finished. He continued his soft rain of kisses, gliding across her temples, her forehead, even the tip of her nose.

"I don't have time for this," she warned.

He just smiled. Probably because her voice had wavered and hadn't sounded convincing at all. She'd sounded as if she *was* affected. Darn it.

He lowered his mouth back to hers, dipped to where only millimeters separated their lips. "My kisses may not affect you, Taylor. But kissing you affects me. My heart is racing and my lungs feel they can't drag in enough air. This weekend wasn't enough. Right or wrong, I need more."

Stop it. Please, just stop talking, her brain warned. Her mouth, unfortunately, didn't say a word. Then again, that might be a good thing because she might admit to how her own heart raced and her own lungs had deflated at his "I want you," at his tender touching of her skin with his lips.

"The anticipation of knowing I'm about to taste your sweet mouth drives me crazy, Taylor," he admitted, his voice low, husky. His gaze lifted to hers. "You drive me crazy."

He drove her crazy, too. She didn't like him and yet...

His lips touched hers. Softly at first, then not so softly, but demanding and masterful. As if he was trying to work through the craziness to some type of satisfied peace.

Only Taylor knew there was no satisfied peace with Slade.

Even after he'd taken her to the pinnacle of pleasure and

she'd thought herself completely sated, all he'd had to do was touch her and she'd been right back to craving more. Crazy. What a perfect description for the desire flooding through her.

The desire to move her lips in response to his.

The desire to wind her arms around his neck.

The desire to press her body fully to his and lean on his strength.

Yep, that was crazy.

She knew better than to lean on a man like Slade. He was a playboy. She'd seen the evidence firsthand for the past year. The fact that he kissed like a dream and his eyes promised her the world didn't mean a thing.

The fact her heart was racing didn't mean a thing.

"I don't like you," she told him the moment his mouth lifted from hers.

"I know," he conceded. "But you want me almost as much as I want you."

Probably more, but she wasn't telling him that.

But kissing him again really wouldn't hurt anything, right? After all, they'd already kissed and she'd done her best not to respond, but she'd have had an easier time stopping the earth's rotation.

Giving in to her need, she stood on tiptoe to press her lips back to his. She should have said something clever like, *Shut up and kiss me*. But talking at all just seemed unnecessary.

Feeding the hunger within her was what was necessary.

Only she knew from experience that kissing Slade wouldn't satisfy her hunger. Instead, his kisses were like an appetizer that made her crave the main course all the more.

She was starved.

Then she recalled how their kiss had started. He'd been proving a point about his kisses affecting her.

She pulled back from him. "I guess I lose."

"Seriously?" Mixed emotions twirled in his blue depths.

"I don't see how sharing that kiss could possibly qualify you as a loser. That kiss makes us both winners."

"If you say so." She took a step back, trying to put some distance between them. "You aren't my type."

"I think we just proved that I'm exactly your type. Do you need a reminder?"

Um, no. She wasn't likely to ever forget that kiss. "That's just sex."

"Sex is a very important part of a relationship."

She rolled her eyes. "Spoken like a true man."

"I am a man, Taylor, but I'll go on record as saying that if you believe sex isn't important to women in a relationship, you're wrong. Sex, whether it be a desire for more of it or less, is an important sharing between a man and a woman."

He was right. But both of her sexual relationships hadn't been about love, just appeasing physical attraction. Kyle had been good, but not like Slade. Not even in the same class.

"What do you know about relationships? You change girlfriends on a monthly basis," she accused, needing to establish some distance between them. "There was the one you went skydiving with, the one you hiked Everest with, the one you did the medical mission trip to Kenya with, the one you—"

"I don't need a recap. I have dated a lot of different women," he interrupted. "But just because my relationships with them didn't last long doesn't mean we didn't have a good relationship while it lasted."

She shook her head. "Again, spoken like a true man. I wonder what the women think."

"I'm still friends with most of them."

She twirled her finger in the air. "Yee-haw for you."

"Are you always so negative?"

"Always. You should stay far away." She waved her fingers at him. "Bye. See you in divorce court."

His expression serious, he said, "Actually, that's what

I'm here to discuss. Have you told anyone we plan to divorce immediately?"

His question had heat infusing her face. Was she supposed to have sent out an office memo? "Only Nina."

"Good," he surprised her by saying.

"Why is that good? What does it even matter? We are
immediately filing for divorce."

"But I think it's better if no one know that. At least, not
until after Christmas."

"What does that matter?"

"Go to dinner with me tonight so we can discuss exactly that."

"I can't. I have Gracie."

He winced, reminding her of how he'd reacted to knowledge of her daughter, to seeing Gracie, to even looking at
her photo. Had he momentarily forgotten?

"If it's the only way you'll agree, then your daughter
can come, too."

She shook her head. Not going to happen. "Wow, with
such sweet talk, how can I resist?"

"Do you want me to sweet-talk you, Taylor? I want you,
but the reason I want to take you to dinner has little to do
with that want."

"Then what does it have to do with?"

"Say yes, and I'll tell you."

Did he think he could manipulate her into going? But then
an idea struck. Slade had enjoyed their sexual rendezvous
where there had just been the two of them and no real-world
responsibilities other than their presentation. He enjoyed
kissing her and seeing her as a woman. She needed to give
him a dose of her real world. In the real world she was the
mother of a rambunctious six-year-old. A six-year-old whom
he obviously had issues with.

She smiled a Cheshire-cat smile. "Okay. We will go to
dinner."

"Okay." Surprise lit his face, and also a look that was

somewhere between relieved that she'd agreed and terrified that she had. "Good. We really do have a lot to talk about. What time can I pick you up?"

"Seven." She gave him her address.

"Okay, then." He took a step back then nodded almost as much to whatever was running through his head as to their conversation. "I'll see you in a little while."

"Taylor, dear, your father's partner said he'd heard a nasty rumor this weekend."

Taylor cringed. No. No. No. She shouldn't have answered the phone. Especially since Slade would be arriving any moment.

"Craig told him that you'd gotten married over the weekend. Your father assured him that was poppycock."

Poppycock? Who said that other than Vivien Anderson?

Then again, perhaps there was no better word for the fact she and Slade had gotten married. Poppycock. Yep, that's what the whole weekend had been. What tonight was.

"Why is the idea of someone marrying me poppycock?"

"Now, Taylor, don't take this the wrong way, but you're not exactly a prize."

Trying not to be hurt, Taylor closed her eyes. Not a prize? Wasn't her mother supposed to see her as the greatest prize a man could win?

"How else is one to take her mother saying she isn't exactly a prize other than the wrong way?"

"Don't go making this about me," her mother warned. "Just tell me you didn't go off and marry someone on a wild whim in Vegas. Surely you know such a union is doomed before it's even started?"

Sure she knew that, but she wasn't admitting to a thing.

"You don't believe in love at first sight?" Why was she being so ornery? Why wasn't she just coming clean that her mother was right and that she'd made a mistake?

"Taylor! Please, tell me you didn't!"

She could lie and tell her that, but her mother's attitude rankled and for once, rather than kowtow, Taylor injected her voice with a perkiness she didn't feel. "It's hardly love at first sight, though. I've known him for a year."

"It's true," her mother gasped, her horror real and thick. "You got married. In Vegas."

Her mother made her words sound as if she had committed the most heinous crime. What else was new? Almost everything she did failed to impress her parents one way or another.

"To a doctor, Mother. He's a very successful man. You should be happy."

But rather than exclaim with joy, her mother rasped, "You're pregnant again, aren't you?"

Taylor cringed. "Do you not think a man might want to marry me just because he wants to be with me?"

Not that that was why Slade had married her, but still.

"In Vegas? Oh, Taylor, you know you wanted a church wedding!"

Had she? Taylor supposed that if she thought about it she would say she had the same wedding fantasies that a lot of women had. A day that was all about her, a gorgeous gown, flowers, a man who loved her with all his heart waiting at the end of an aisle. Not necessarily in a church, but she doubted a place named after the North Pole would have made the top one hundred.

"Vegas was much more exciting, Mom. Not everyone gets married by Santa Claus." Okay, in reality, being married by a minister in a furry red suit wasn't on her mom's top one hundred list either.

"Please, tell me you are joking."

"In a gingerbread house rather than a church. There were real elves and everything." She was bad, knew she was being bad, but she so didn't need her mother condemning her right now. She had enough of her own regrets. "It was a really unique ceremony."

"Your father is going to be so disappointed that he didn't get to walk you down the aisle."

Her mother was so disappointed she didn't get to have the huge social-club reception to show off to all her friends. Her father? She thought about the stern businessman who, although devout and good, wasn't an overly emotional man. Perhaps her mother knew a side she didn't. Perhaps her father really did want to walk his only child down the aisle. Maybe she'd stolen that experience from him, too.

Taylor felt a twinge of remorse. Her parents had been good parents, had sent her to the best schools, had made sure she'd had the best advantages in life, had always been there if she'd physically needed something. Was it their fault she'd constantly been a disappointment to them? That she'd failed them miserably when she'd gotten pregnant in medical school? That she'd accidentally gotten married in Vegas?

"I'll reserve the club for a reception." Her mother confirmed Taylor's earlier thoughts. "With the holidays, I may have to call in several favors to get the main ballroom, but I'll do my best."

"Mom, I don't need or want a wedding reception." She didn't even want the marriage.

"Nonsense. All our friends and family will be offended if they don't get to share in such an important event."

Taylor took a deep breath. Several of her coworkers had suggested throwing her a bridal shower. She'd put them off with claims of the holidays being so busy.

"Mom, it isn't fair to your club to make them shuffle around their holiday schedule to fit in a reception."

"But—"

"No buts. I have so much going on right now with Gracie, the holidays, with work."

"Fine," her mother conceded. "I'll book the first thing available for after the holidays."

Planning a reception for after the holidays was as useless as planning one for before the holidays. Unless one gave receptions to celebrate the dissolution of one's impromptu Vegas vows?

Taylor tried arguing with her mother, but to no avail as Vivien cut the conversation short. No doubt to call to book her club.

Was it wrong that she had given Gracie a glass of soda prior to Slade's arrival? That she wanted Gracie in full-chatter, full-tilt mode? That she wanted to push Slade out of his comfort zone? To play on all his worst fears about being around a kid? For him to see her as a woman who was a mother who had real-world responsibilities and not as the woman he'd slept with in Vegas?

"Mommy!" Gracie called when the doorbell rang. She jumped up and down, her blond ponytail swishing wildly. "He's here. He's here."

She'd told Gracie that a friend from work was coming to take them to Pippa's Pizza Palace. Gracie had been ecstatic because they usually only went to the designed-for-kids restaurant for birthday parties or special occasions.

Knowing she wasn't supposed to unlock the latch, Gracie bounced back and forth in front of the foyer door. Taylor had her step aside so she could let Slade in.

When she swung the door open, he gave her a wary smile that made her question how long he had been standing out there on her porch.

"Hey."

"Hey, yourself," she flung back, moving back so he could enter the foyer. "Gracie, do you remember Dr. Sain? You met him briefly at the airport."

"I remember." Gracie beamed at him, dancing around at his feet. "He took care of Vegas."

Oh, he'd taken care of Vegas all right. Her daughter meant the bear, but Taylor couldn't help but think of the real ways Slade had taken care of Vegas. She'd hoped Gracie would rename her bear, but the name had stuck so far.

Vegas had bumped Foxy as Gracie's favorite toy and she kept the bear close.

"That's right. Let's grab your coat and be off so we can get you to bed at a decent time for school tomorrow."

Gracie ran to the living room where her jacket and bear lay on the sofa.

Slade's gaze followed the bouncing little girl out of the room, then shifted to Taylor. "You look great."

Taylor laughed at Slade's compliment. She'd purposely put on an old sweatshirt and jeans, scrubbed her face clean and pulled her hair into a ponytail. Great wasn't the right adjective by any use of the word. Neither was it the adjective she'd use to describe how he looked. He looked as if he'd rather be anywhere other than here.

"Got them," Gracie announced proudly when she returned with her jacket and bear.

Her daughter handed her bear to Slade while Taylor made a great production of helping Gracie into her coat. Let him realize firsthand why she had no time for playboys.

"Be careful with her," Gracie warned him. "She is a delicate princess and has to be treated royally. She would probably like it if you pretended to be a prince come to rescue her."

What popped out of Gracie's mouth had stopped surprising Taylor long ago. Her daughter was brilliant and readily got people to do her bidding. Slade, despite whatever was bugging him, was no exception, and whatever the problem had been he seemed to have overcome it, at least for the moment.

"Who says I'm not really a prince?" he asked, bending to Gracie's level. He held the bear to where he was staring into her painted plastic eyes. "Vegas, did you forget to tell Gracie that I am Prince Charming come to sweep the two most beautiful girls in the world off their feet?"

Gracie's eyes widened. "She did forget to tell me."

"Vegas," he scolded the bear with a gentle click of his tongue. "How could you forget something so important?"

Taylor rolled her eyes, wondering if she'd made a hor-rible mistake in letting her daughter spend time with Slade. She'd expected him not to want to deal with a six-year-old girl, for them to have a short evening with Slade and Gracie not having time to form any attachments. What she hadn't counted on was Slade actually playing along with Gracie's imaginings. She liked that and she didn't need anything else to like about the man.

"Let's go," she growled, irritated at herself. "I'm hungry."

"Uh-oh, Vegas." Slade's voice sounded concerned. "Prin-cess Taylor has spoken and we must do her bidding."

Gracie giggled. "She's not Princess Taylor. She's Queen Mommy."

Good girl, Gracie. Remind him of my real role in life. The most important role in her life. That of loving and rais-ing her daughter to the best of her ability.

Even if she had loaded her with sugar prior to his arrival.

As if she'd read her mind, Gracie started bouncing again. "Mommy let me and Vegas have soda pop!"

Hmm, maybe she should have let Gracie in on the fact that she hadn't wanted that little tidbit shared.

Slade just looked at her, raised his brow, then grinned, his stress seeming to melt away with that revelation. "Wow. It must be a special night if she let you have soda."

Gracie nodded. "It is. We're going to Pippa's Pizza Palace."

"Pippa's Pizza Palace?" Slade's gaze went to Taylor for confirmation. She nodded.

"Well," he continued, giving Taylor a look that said he knew exactly what she was up to. "It is a palace, so of course that's where princes and princesses should go."

Ha. Wasn't he in for a surprise if he expected any kind of royal treatment at Pippa's Pizza Palace. Overpriced pizza, kiddie rides and games were hardly regal.

Totally enamored, Gracie slipped her hand into Tay-lor's and headed out the front door. "Vegas is really excited about going to Pippa's Pizza Palace. She wants her very own crown."

"Then her very own crown she shall have," Slade promised. "After all, she is a very special princess who traveled from far, far away."

Taylor followed Slade to his car.

"Let's load you up into your chariot," he suggested to Gracie. He looked more confident than he had when he'd first arrived. Too bad he was about to have his bubble burst.

Also having figured out there was a problem, Gracie glanced up at Taylor in question. Taylor had to fight to hide her smile.

"We should take my car instead," she suggested from behind him, watching his face closely.

"Why?"

"I think you're forgetting something. Princess Gracie is only six and has to be in a children's car seat."

His expression was priceless. "Is there a seat we can just put in mine?"

Taylor hesitated a brief moment, then shook her head. "Nina has my extra seat and the one in my van is built-in."

"Your van?"

"I drive a minivan. That's what we soccer moms do."

She was driving her point home that they were on opposite ends of the spectrum. Whatever he was thinking, he didn't say anything to her, just grinned at Gracie as if he found dealing with her easier than Taylor at the moment. "You play soccer? I love soccer!"

Gracie nodded at her new hero.

"What position do you play?"

Gracie shrugged and glanced at Taylor for an answer.

"You're a forward."

"A forward," Gracie told him, puffing out her tiny chest as she did.

"That's a great position," he praised, then turned to Taylor. "Can we take your minivan instead of my car?"

She glanced toward his car. She'd seen the sporty coupe in the parking lot at the hospital, knew that's what he drove. The expensive car fit him and was perfect no doubt for impressing the women he dated.

Seven years ago Taylor would have been impressed, too. Now flashy toys and good looks didn't impress her that much. What was on the inside of a man, his morals and his character, that's what she valued. Not that Slade would have guessed that after their wild Vegas rendezvous. He probably thought deep down she was no different from the other women who had been in and out of his life.

Only as she unlocked her garage door she couldn't quite convince herself that Slade saw her the same way as the other women he'd dated.

He hadn't married any of the other women in his life.

Sure, they'd married on a silly lust-fueled Vegas whim, but they had married.

He stood next to her, taking in each step of Gracie being safely buckled into her seat. Once Taylor was confident Gracie was properly buckled in, she handed her van keys to him.

"You're going to let me drive?" he asked, obviously surprised.

"Boys are supposed to drive," Gracie piped up from her seat.

"Don't ever let any guy tell you he's supposed to drive. If you want to drive, drive."

Gracie giggled. "I don't know how to drive."

"What?" He pretended shock. "Well, I guess princesses should be chauffeured around anyway."

Taylor watched their interaction with suspicious eyes. Of course Slade was on his best behavior. She'd thought being around Gracie would make him see her as a mom and not as the woman he'd spent the weekend with in Vegas. Perhaps she'd made a mistake.

Then again, the night was young.

CHAPTER EIGHT

Slade wrapped his fingers around Taylor's keys, watched the play of emotions across her face, then opened the passenger door for her.

"Your chariot awaits, Queen Taylor." He made a production of bowing, and earned claps and praise from Gracie. Not that he'd had much experience around kids, or even wanted that experience, but he admitted he enjoyed her honest reactions to the things he said and did.

"This is my chariot, too," the little girl informed him. "My royal chariot. For me and Princess Vegas."

"Absolutely."

Taylor rolled her eyes. She climbed into the front passenger seat and he shut the door, winked at Gracie, who winked back, then he slid her door closed, too.

So far, so good. Which he didn't think was supposed to be the case since even in his limited experience he knew sodas hyped most kids. He'd bet anything Taylor was one of those moms who limited her daughter's sweets. Tonight was not supposed to be a success. Too bad. He was determined it would be. He had a proposal to make. One that had been nagging at him from the moment it had occurred to him. One he hoped Taylor would agree to.

Gracie chatted nonstop, mostly about Santa and Christmas, on the drive to Pippa's Pizza Palace, which, despite the castle-shaped sign, didn't look like a place fit for a princess to eat. The building was a bit run-down and the parking lot needed repaving. Still, when they got inside, the interior was colorful and clean, if dated.

Gracie obviously didn't care. First getting a nod from her mother, she took off toward a row of machines and kiddie rides on the opposite side of the large open room.

Before they had placed their order Gracie was back, asking if she could have some coins.

"Let's get dinner ordered first."

"I'm not hungry," Gracie insisted, tugging on her mother's hand. "Can I play now?"

Taylor shook her head. "Not until you've eaten."

Gracie's lower lip drooped, and her shoulders sagged to where she looked like a deflated tire. "Do I have to?"

Taylor nodded, then, while Gracie ran back over to watch one of the video-game monitors, she turned to the cashier, placed an order for a small cheese pizza, a salad, a lemon water and a juice. The cashier glanced toward Slade, but Taylor shook her head.

"Our orders are separate."

"You'll have to excuse my wife. She doesn't understand the concept of 'date night,'" Slade explained to the cashier. "I will pay for their order and mine."

"No."

"Yes. Get us a table, please, and I'll finish here, wifey."

"I didn't say yes so you could buy dinner or call me 'wifey.'"

"Odd, because I did ask you to dinner so I could buy your dinner."

She pursed her lips, looking as if she'd like to argue, but instead she did as he'd suggested. He watched her walk over to a clean booth and put her purse on the seat. Then he turned back to the cashier and completed the order, along with purchasing some coins for Gracie.

"You didn't have to buy coins," Taylor said when he slid into the booth with his huge stash.

"Because we came to the Pippa's Pizza Palace to watch other kids play?"

"We came to eat."

"Pretty sure Gracie would be disappointed if she only gets to eat." As he said the words realization hit. "Unless that's your plan?" He studied her, noting her pink cheeks. "You'd like tonight to be a failure so you can add it to your reasons why we don't belong together?"

"We don't belong together." She made it sound like a disease. "I thought we agreed on that."

"We do."

"Then our being here makes no sense."

He glanced toward where Gracie covetously watched two kids whacking at clowns popping up from the top of a machine shaped like a cannon.

"Actually, our being together does make sense short-term." He needed to explain his proposal, but didn't get the chance as Gracie skipped back to their table.

"Mommy, after I eat, can I hit the clowns, too?" Gracie's eyes sparkled, her cheeks glowed and her voice held excitement.

"I'm not sure how I feel about a game where you beat up poor defenseless clowns," Taylor mused, smiling at her Mini-Me.

"Are you kidding me? Clowns are some scary business. We should both help just to be sure we get them all."

Giving Slade a beatific grin, Gracie nodded enthusiastically. "You should!"

"Don't tell me you are afraid of clowns?" Taylor asked, eyeing him with a slight smile.

"Terrified," he admitted, half-serious. He'd never been one of those kids who liked clowns. Maybe he'd watched one too many scary movies involving weirdos in clown suits.

"I'm not scared of clowns," Gracie announced, taking his hand. "Mommy's not either. We'll protect you."

"Phew. Thanks."

"Do you want to watch with me? We could look at the other games and pick out ones to play," she suggested, her eyes big and pleading.

Slade glanced toward Taylor to get her permission. Should he wait until after Gracie had eaten?

Taylor nodded. "I'm pretty sure that the games haven't changed since the last time we were here, but you should definitely show Dr. Sain all your favorite ones."

"You can come too, Mommy."

Taylor shook her head. "You two go ahead. Mommy will watch for our food. Plus, I have a phone call to make."

Gracie tugged on Slade's hand. "Come on. You have got to see the frog game! It's amazing."

Slade gave one last look toward Taylor, who, he knew, had purposely set him up to go off alone to supervise Gracie, then he devoted his attention to the child holding his hand. Something about her warm little hand gripping his, about the excitement with which she spoke, made him want to pick her up and hug her. Getting attached would be nothing short of stupid. Yet he'd jumped at the chance to spend time with Taylor. So he could ask her a favor. Nothing more. Not really.

If she'd agree to a no-strings affair, he'd jump at that chance, too. Too bad he knew she'd never offer that.

"Amazing?" he asked the girl, forcing his mind away from Taylor. "The frog game?"

Gracie nodded with great emphasis. "Amazing."

"Okay, let's go see this amazing frog game."

He let the little girl lead him over to a game where you had to squirt water onto a lily pad to make a frog move from the lily pad to where a fly was. Interesting.

But not interesting enough to keep his gaze from wandering back to the woman sitting in the booth, talking on her cellular phone. She laughed at something said, then glanced his way, caught him looking at her and frowned.

"Rolling the balls is my favorite game, but I'm not very good," Gracie informed him, tugging on his hands to take him away from the frog game and farther into the maze of games. "Mommy is really good."

She stopped in front of a row of Skee-Ball lanes.

Slade glanced over at the booth where Taylor sat, talking on her cellular phone, smiling and laughing. Her face was relaxed, beautiful, almost carefree. Who was she talking to? She'd told him she wasn't having sex with anyone, but had she been dating? He'd never asked if there was someone special in her life. There couldn't have been anyone too special or she wouldn't have married him, wouldn't have had sex with him.

Gracie continued to talk about her mother's awesomeness at Skee-Ball.

Slade smiled down at the excited little girl. "Your mommy likes to play this game?"

Gracie nodded. "It's her favorite. She's really good. She gets lots of tickets, but she always gives them to me to get the prize." The little girl gave him a pointed look, wanting to be sure he knew that giving her the tickets was the right thing to do.

Slade's gaze wandered back to Taylor. She twirled a loose strand of hair around her finger and still talked animatedly to whoever she was on the phone with. Jealousy wasn't a pretty thing and he was definitely jealous. He wanted her smiling and laughing like that with him, the way they had on the night they'd gotten married.

"That's nice of her."

Gracie nodded. "She's a nice mommy. My friend Sarah Beth, her mommy isn't nice." Gracie wrinkled her nose and looked so much like Taylor, Slade couldn't suppress the melting of his heart. There might be traits of her father present in Gracie, but when Slade looked at the little girl all he saw was a miniature version of Taylor.

"She screams and cries a lot," Gracie continued, her face and hand movements dramatic.

Slade wasn't exactly sure how he was supposed to respond, but decided a response wasn't necessary because Gracie kept right on talking and waving her hands.

"Sarah Beth says it's because she's pregnant and the baby in her belly kicks her a lot. Sarah Beth's daddy says this baby is going to be a soccer player, too. Sarah Beth is on my soccer team, but soccer season won't start back till this spring. You should come watch my games. I am very good. Mommy tells me so."

Slade took a breath for Gracie because she seemed too busy chatting to breathe. But she must have been sneaking breaths in somewhere because she kept going without being the slightest bit winded, pointing out several other games that she really hoped to play when they finished eating.

"Do you have kids?"

Gracie's random question in the middle of her rundown of her classmates caught him off guard. He shook his head.

"No, I don't have kids." For the first time in his life he almost felt as if he was lacking something by that answer. Perhaps it was the sad little look Gracie gave him, as if she was offering him comfort that he didn't.

"Are you married?"

While he racked his brain for a way to answer honestly without telling her anything her mother wasn't ready for her to know, Gracie leapt up and down.

"Yummy!" she called, grabbing his hand and not waiting for an answer when she spotted their food being delivered to the table. "Pizza. I'm a pizza-eating machine."

She made a pretense of gobbling air bites.

"Me, too," he agreed, grateful for the distraction as they headed back to the table.

"Sorry, Nina, but I've got to go. I'll talk with you tomorrow at work." She paused while the person on the other end of the phone line said something. "Okay, see you then. Have a good night."

"Nina doing okay?" he asked, to verify that she'd been talking to her best friend. He really didn't like the green flowing through his veins, the green that had flowed through his veins at the thought that there might be someone in Taylor's life. It shouldn't matter. If anything, he should want her to have someone in her life who could give her all the things she wanted for her and Gracie. All the things they deserved. It was probably some natural instinct for him to feel jealousy where Taylor was concerned. After all, she was his wife.

"She checked on Mrs. Jamison for me. They admitted her overnight for observation, but otherwise she's good."

"Mr. Slade is going to play games with me when we finish eating," Gracie announced while Taylor squirted hand sanitizer onto her tiny hands. "He's going to come to watch me and Sarah Beth play soccer this spring, too."

Slade hadn't really agreed to that, but he wasn't going to correct the child's claim. Catching Taylor's glare, he should have, though. She offered Slade the bottle and he took it, their hands brushing against each other. Zings shot up his arm. How could a single touch cause such a wave of awareness throughout his entire body?

He glanced at her to see if she'd felt the electricity that had zapped him, but she refused to look at him, her focus totally on her daughter as she put a slice of pizza onto a colorful paper plate.

"Mmm, pizza," Gracie said, continuing to talk a mile a minute.

Slade handed the sanitizer back to Taylor and found it interesting that she managed to take the bottle without a single touch of their skin this time. Had that been intentional?

"What is on your pizza, Mr. Slade, because I only like cheese pizza." Gracie took a big bite of her pizza to prove her point.

"I got a little of everything on mine," he told her, reaching for a slice of the house special. He eyed the rather bland-looking salad Taylor had ordered. "You want a slice? I'll share."

She shook her head. "I'll finish off what Gracie doesn't eat of her pizza."

"Cheese is your favorite?"

"No, but she won't be able to eat it all."

"I will be able to eat it all," Gracie corrected her. "I'm starved." She sucked in her tiny belly and lifted her shirt to show Taylor.

Taylor smiled at her daughter and a piece of Slade's heart cracked at the love that showed in her eyes, a love he hadn't seen in years. That's what he'd lost when his mother had died, why he'd dedicated his life to breast-cancer research, why he was determined to prevent other kids from losing the same.

"Guess you better get to eating, then, before you blow away, hungry girl. But not too big bites, please," Taylor added, when Gracie took a huge mouthful, oblivious to the emotional turmoil playing out in Slade's head.

Gracie ate a slice, then eyed the games. "I'm full. Can I go play now?"

"You can, but we're not finished eating so it'll be a few minutes before we join you. Stay where I can see you."

"Okay." Gracie looked at Slade. "Hurry so I can show you how good I am at the frog game. I will beat you."

Slade watched her bounce back over to the games. "She's precious."

"I think so."

"But you didn't want me to think so?"

"I didn't say that."

"You didn't have to. You gave her soda."

She sucked in her lower lip. "So?" she challenged. "Lots of kids drink soda."

"But you don't normally give Gracie soda."

"Not usually," she admitted, impressing him that she'd been honest. He got the impression Taylor was an honest person who truly tried to live her life to a high standard.

Was that something her parents had instilled in her or just who she innately was? Speaking of honesty...

"Gracie asked me if I was married."

Taylor's stomach sank. Had Slade told Gracie they'd married? "What did you tell her?"

"Not what you apparently think I did."

Which didn't really tell her a whole lot. "Then what did you say?"

He set another piece of pizza on his paper plate. "I didn't answer because we were saved by the pizza arriving."

She watched him take a bite of the loaded pizza. Her stomach growled in protest at her salad.

"I've changed my mind about telling her. I'll tell her when she's older, when she'll understand better."

He paused with his pizza midway to his mouth, an odd gleam in his eyes. "Do I embarrass you, Taylor?"

"What?"

"I'm just curious because you haven't wanted anyone to know that you married me. I was curious if you were ashamed of me."

Was that what he thought? If anything, he should be ashamed of her. She was the one who was so different from the women he'd dated. "Of course not. That's ridiculous."

As if he were no longer hungry, he set the pizza back on his plate. "Is it?"

"Of course. If I was embarrassed by you I would not have agreed to go to dinner with you tonight."

"But dinner wasn't supposed to be a success. Dinner was supposed to shove in my face that you aren't a carefree woman who can have an affair until our divorce is final."

Busted. "I didn't say that."

"You didn't have to," he pointed out, leaning slightly across the table toward her. "I have a proposal to make."

A proposal? Her stomach knotting, she eyed him suspiciously.

"Let's not tell anyone that we plan to divorce until after the holidays."

Taylor swallowed back what she was positive wasn't disappointment because she hadn't really expected him to propose they continue their weekend fling yet again.

"I can't see what the point would be," she told him, even if staring at him across the table made her want to drag him under the table and... She swallowed again.

"It would make things easier at work if we waited."

Taylor thought back on her conversation with her mother. Now there was a buzz killer. The thought of telling her that she'd been planning her divorce less than twenty-four hours after saying "I do" turned her stomach.

He picked at the edge of his paper plate then met her gaze again. "Plus, keeping the truth quiet would make things better for my family. I don't celebrate Christmas, but they do. I'd rather not ruin their holidays by having them worried that I'm facing divorce in the New Year."

He didn't celebrate Christmas? She wondered why, not liking the way her heart raced at how he was looking at her, at how her heart broke that he missed out on the joys of the holidays.

"I don't want anyone to know that our marriage isn't real," he admitted, his sincerity drawing her further into the spell he cast with such seeming effortlessness. "I know you've told Nina, but she wouldn't say anything if you asked her not to."

"You've not told anyone?"

"No. I started to tell my dad last night, but I couldn't do it. He's already worried that I've gotten married so suddenly that I just didn't have the heart to tell him."

She closed her eyes. She couldn't condemn him for not telling his father. After all, she hadn't set her mother straight. Still...

Was she strong enough to pretend they were happily married? He affected her as no other man ever had, made

her heart race and her body ache, made her heart long for
dreams that had been shattered long ago. He made her want
and feel all kinds of scary emotions.

"I'm sorry. I just don't think I can do pretend."

"Sure you can. We did pretend in Vegas and it was amazing."

"That was different and you know it."

He considered her a moment then leaned toward her, his
face only inches from hers as his gaze dropped to her lips,
hesitated, then lifted back to her eyes in challenge. "Play
me for it."

She couldn't breathe. Couldn't hear for the pounding of
her chest. "What?" she choked out.

His grin was lethal, warning her she should just say no
to whatever he was offering. "Play me to decide if we tell
everyone now or wait until after the holidays."

Was it just her or had someone cranked up the heat in
Pippa's Pizza Palace? Surely the thermometer was set on
flaming-inferno mode. "That's ridiculous."

"Be that as it may, I'm serious." His gaze didn't waver
from hers. Could he see that she was sweating? Would it be
too obvious if she fanned her face?

"Why would I agree?"

"Because, if you really think about it, it's the right thing
for both of us. But if you insist otherwise, if you win, I will
give you what you say you want. I'll leave you alone and
we'll go back to the way things were before Vegas. Plus, I
will quit trying to engage you in conversation or asking you
to dinner or even acknowledging that you exist."

His smile should have her running, but instead she considered what he'd said. How could she not when she could
feel his breath against her lips? Or was she just imagining
the soft caress that made her want to lean in and close the
gap between them?

She frowned and leaned as far back in her seat as she

could without looking as if she was auditioning for a human contortionist act.

"I'll quit trying to convince you to let me strip you naked and repeat all the naughty things we did last weekend, even though I will probably still be thinking about those things and wanting them, wanting you."

Her heart squeezed and she felt a little panicky at the thought of what he'd promised, of what he'd said. Not panic. Excitement. Anticipation. Slade leaving her alone was what she wanted. What she needed. She wasn't strong, and what if she gave in to the physical sparks that burned so potently between them? Especially when he kept saying he wanted her? What if he kissed her and she forgot everything but the fact that she was a woman and he made her glad of it? What if she acknowledged that he hadn't epically failed with being around her daughter tonight?

Play a game, win and he'd back off trying to convince her to have an affair destined to lead nowhere but to heartache for her. That's what she needed. Wanted. So what was the catch? "Not that I'm agreeing to anything, but what would we play?"

"Your choice."

Her choice? "Let me get this straight. I get to pick the game and if I win, you avoid me at all costs? No changing your mind?"

"Yes," he agreed, not looking in the slightest worried. "But if I win you will give me a month of pretending to be happily married and if you happen to decide you aren't opposed to continuing our physical relationship, well, that would be an added perk."

She ignored the little voice inside her head reminding her of the last time he'd *proved* something to her, of just how tempting she found that added perk. "A month?"

"A month. That puts us at New Year."

She bit the inside of her lip. She didn't really think he could beat her at Skee-Ball, but a month…

This was crazy. He was crazy. Why was she even considering his suggestion?

"I don't want my daughter hurt."

His blue eyes twinkling, he looked more relaxed than he had all evening. "So you admit even before we start that I'd win?"

She lifted her chin a notch. "I'm not admitting anything."

His grin was wicked. "But you aren't denying that I'd win either."

She glanced over at her daughter, who was watching another child play a coin-toss game. Her gaze lit on the Skee-Ball lanes. She could do this. She could beat him, remove all temptation and just move past the events of the past weekend. It's what she needed for her sanity because being around him made her crazy.

"Any game?"

His smile broadened. "Any game."

"Skee-Ball."

He didn't hesitate, just nodded. "Best of five?"

Why had the air in the room gotten so thin?

"Best of five," she agreed, wondering what she'd just agreed to. Not that it mattered. She couldn't recall the last time she'd lost at Skee-Ball.

"We both get a warm-up game?"

She shook her head. She just wanted to get this over with. "I don't need a warm-up game."

He looked impressed. "Okay. But don't say I didn't offer."

Taylor smiled. "No changing your mind when you lose. We'll tell everyone the truth and you'll leave me alone at all times. No looks, no flirting, no daring me into kisses, no anything. You'll stay completely away from me. Tonight will be the last time I have to deal with you."

"No changing your mind when you lose," he countered. "You agree to a month of pretending to be happily married to me, spending time with me, and tolerating my looks, flirts and dares to kiss. Although, in private, win or lose, you call

the shots and I'll honor your wishes. In January, we'll an-
nounce our divorce plans and go our separate ways."

There went her throat, gulping again. "If I refuse to
play?"

"Then regardless of what we tell others about our marriage, I will actively pursue what I want, which is you in
my bed."

Panic tightened her throat for a brief second, then she
reminded herself that he was not going to win.

"Unless you're willing to admit that you want me as much
as I want you, you have nothing to lose by playing me."

No way was she admitting that to him. Sure, there was
no way he couldn't know how he'd made her body explode
and implode and reload over and over in Vegas, but she was
not admitting a thing.

"You're right. Because I won't lose."

Not looking in the slightest intimidated by her bravado,
he grinned. "Such confidence. I like it."

She picked up a piece of Gracie's leftover cheese pizza
and took a bite. "I'm good at Skee-Ball."

He watched her eat, and if he was attempting to hide
that eyeing her mouth gave him pleasure he failed. "Gracie
mentioned that."

Yet he'd agreed. That threw her. "You knew and you still
let me pick which game we played? Do you want to lose? Is
this some kind of sick joke?"

"In case you haven't figured this out yet, despite how
many times I've told you, I want you. And for the record
I don't like to lose or fail at anything. Something we have
in common."

When she just stared blankly at him, he elaborated. "Our
competitive spirit."

She didn't think she had a competitive spirit, but there
was something about the man that made her want to get one
up on him. Plus, she wasn't 100 percent sure he wasn't just
toying with her. Maybe he sensed how much she struggled

with her attraction to him and out of boredom he planned to prove his point on that score as well.

Either way, all she had to do was win and, whatever his motive, it would be a moot point.

CHAPTER NINE

AT GRACIE'S ENCOURAGEMENT, Taylor and Slade played three of the frog games first. Gracie won each time. They also played several of the other electronic games, including whacking the clowns.

Hearing Gracie, seeing the joy on her daughter's face at their antics, eased Taylor's nerves.

Knowing that she would win, that Slade would quit pursuing their physical relationship, helped calm her fear of how he made her long for things she shouldn't.

He didn't seem nervous. He'd been laughing and mostly at ease with Gracie, the kiddie games and with the whole chaos of Pippa's Pizza Palace. Every once in a while she'd catch him responding a little awkwardly to Gracie's exuberance, but otherwise he'd impressed her.

"Ready to win Gracie a bunch of tickets?" His eyes sparkled with challenge.

"Oh, yeah." She was ready to get the game over so they could go home. Not that she wasn't having fun. Of course she was having fun. Slade was a fun guy. Fun wasn't the problem. But he wasn't what she wanted in a man, in a father for Gracie. He'd hurt her, hurt Gracie, if she gave him the chance. That was the problem. Why she'd needed a stronger barrier to her feelings to begin with.

That plan sure had backfired. Gracie hung on to his every word and wanted him beside her for each game they played.

She'd even caught her daughter batting her lashes at Slade. The man was a charmer. Age didn't matter. Females flocked to him and her daughter was no exception.

She ran her gaze over his handsome profile and admitted that he was definitely flock worthy. He made her want to flock, too. If only…

He turned, caught her watching him and grinned.

Taylor rolled her eyes. No need to give him a bigger ego than he already had. If he knew how much she thought about him, about their wedding night and how she wished the way he'd kissed her had been real and that he wanted a month with her to win her heart rather than to have an affair, he'd definitely tease her. Likely, he'd break her heart if given the chance. That's why she needed to accept his challenge, to beat him at his own game, so he'd back off from pursuing her and hopefully she'd walk away from their marriage without any mortal wounds.

Gracie took the center lane and they watched her play a game prior to their dropping coins into the next lane.

"You go first," she offered.

Slade shook his head. "Ladies first."

Taylor shrugged, then picked up a ball and smoothly rolled it down the lane. It dropped effortlessly into the highest point slot.

"Oh, yeah!"

Gracie high-fived her.

Slade nodded in approval. "Nice."

Unfortunately, her next two dropped into the next to highest point level slot. Frustrated that she wasn't rolling a perfect game, the remainder went into the same just-below-perfect slot until she ran out of balls.

Her score wasn't her highest, but it wasn't bad. She stepped aside. "Your turn."

"Do you want to do all five of your games first, keep a score tally and then me go?"

She shook her head. "I thought we were going to play

against each other and have winners each time. The best of
five, remember?"

"Either way is fine."

He dropped more coins into the slot. A new set of balls
rolled down. Slade picked one up, rolled it down the lane,
and plopped it into the highest point slot.

When he repeatedly dropped the balls into the same slot,
Taylor began to feel clammy.

"You're pretty good."

He rolled the remainder of his balls. "I dated a girl in
high school who worked in a place like this. I killed a lot of
time playing this game while waiting for her shift to finish."

His rolls didn't remain perfect, but his final score was
higher than Taylor's.

Gracie jumped up and down, clapping. "You're good, Mr.
Slade! You beat Mommy. Look at all those tickets."

Slade tore off the long string of tickets. "These are for
you, princess. We'll have you more in just a few."

"Yay," she squealed, waving the tickets around.

"Okay, then," Taylor said, her palms sweating. Of course
he'd dated someone who'd worked at a place that had Skee-
Ball lanes. He'd probably dated a professional Skee-Ball
player and coach, too. If there was an international Skee-Ball
game, he'd probably won gold. Urgh. "I guess it's my turn."

"That it is." Slade looked as if he was having the time of
his life. The fink.

Taylor started the new game and took her time to make
sure she sank the balls into the highest scoring slot. She
did well and upped her score by forty points, which would
have beaten Slade in the previous game. She smiled as she
stepped back.

Excited, Gracie gathered the tickets the machine was
spitting out.

"Nice job," Slade agreed, obviously not concerned. He
started his game and tied her score with almost effort-
less ease.

"Hmmm," he mused. "We didn't discuss how to handle a tied score."

Annoyed at how calm he was, she stretched her arms over her shoulders. She just needed to loosen up a little to beat him. "We'll just keep playing. One tied game may not make a difference."

But Slade tied her next two scores. Gracie was ecstatic. Taylor was not. Three ties and he'd won the first game. She had to win this next one.

Putting all her focus into the game, she picked up her first ball and dropped it into the highest point slot. Yes. She repeated that time and again, the ball only dropping into a lower slot once. An almost perfect game. It was the highest score of the night.

Finally! Breathing much easier, she glanced at Slade. "Your turn."

"That's a pretty high score. What happens if I tie you or get a higher score?"

"You won't," she said dismissively, more for her benefit than his.

His lips twitched. "But if I did?"

"You would win because you won that first game."

"If I don't tie you?"

"We'd have to play a sixth game to break the tied score."

"I just wanted to be clear."

Slade rolled the ball and it dropped perfectly into the highest point slot. Each and every time. He only had one more to have a perfect game. He'd be up two wins to her none. If he tied her, he'd still win. Only if his ball dropped into a lower point slot would she win. Even then, they'd possibly have to play a tiebreaker. Knots twisted her stomach.

He surprised her by holding out the ball.

"Gracie, would you like to roll my last ball?"

The little girl, who had been enthusiastically gathering tickets, jumped up and down and nodded, her ponytail bouncing almost as excitedly as she had been. "I would."

He handed Gracie the ball and the little girl looked up at him, suddenly uncertain. "Will you help me, Mr. Slade? I want to do good and get more tickets."

Taylor wasn't sure anyone could resist such a sweet, innocent plea, and Slade was no exception. He stood behind Gracie, helped position her body just so, pulled her arm back and helped guide her through the motions. Gracie let go and the ball dropped into the second from highest slot, tying Taylor's score.

Taylor's knees almost gave way beneath her. No.

"That was good!" Eyes wide, Gracie jumped up and down, superenergized about her success.

Slade picked her up and twirled her around. "Princess, you are amazing!"

She giggled and patted his cheeks. "Did we win?"

He nodded. "We did win. We make a good team."

"Yea." Gracie high-fived him. "Princes and princesses always make good teams."

Taylor watched them, wondering at the doomed feeling in her gut, wondering at the emotional pangs at how her daughter was so quickly responding to Slade.

With a suddenly serious expression Gracie looked up at Taylor with her big green eyes. "You're not mad 'cause I helped Mr. Slade win, are you, Mommy?"

Oops. Her silence had gotten her daughter's attention. Oh, Slade was slick. He'd used her daughter against her. If she showed disappointment, Gracie would think her a poor sport.

Pasting a smile on her face, Taylor gestured to the long strand of tickets. "Nope. I think with as awesome as you just did you're going to run the machines out of tickets. Did you see all those?"

"Wow." Gracie's eyes grew large. "I'm going to get a stuffed monkey."

"A what?"

Gracie pointed to where the prize booth was. Hanging

from the ceiling was a big green stuffed monkey with a yellow banana in his hand. "I want him."

Okay. "How many tickets does he take?"

Gracie shrugged.

"Let's find out." While Gracie and Slade ran their tickets through a counter, Taylor asked the teenaged cashier at the booth how many were needed for the monkey.

"That many?"

The boy nodded.

"Mommy, we have over a thousand tickets!"

"We're going to need them."

Slade grinned. "Takes that many for a big green monkey, huh?"

Ignoring his expression, she told him.

He whistled. "Expensive monkey."

"He's worth it," Gracie assured them, eyeing the monkey with longing. "He's the king of the jungle and has been trapped up there for months and months. He needs to get back to his kingdom."

Slade looked intrigued. "He does?"

All seriousness and in full Gracie-imagination mode, she nodded. "Plus, he has to find a princess to go to the jungle with him and lead his people."

"You're a princess," Slade reminded her, getting into Gracie's active imaginings.

"I'm a princess," Gracie agreed with a *duh* expression. "But he's going to fall in love with Princess Vegas." She took on a worried expression. "Let's hope she likes big green monkeys because not all princesses do, even though they are so cute and cuddly."

Slade's gaze lifted to Taylor's and despite still reeling inside that he'd won, that he'd brought Gracie onto his side, she smiled at his rather bewildered, overwhelmed, yet totally enamored expression.

Probably a similar expression to the one she wore that for

the next month she would be pretending to be happily married to Slade and he'd be actively pursuing an affair with her.

An affair she couldn't afford emotionally.

"I want the biggest tree they have," Gracie informed Slade and Taylor as they pulled up to the Christmas-tree lot in Taylor's van the following Friday evening. "A gigantic one so I can climb high into the sky!"

"Christmas trees aren't for climbing."

Gracie scrunched her face at her mother's comment. "They should be. Christmas would be so much fun if I could climb the tree." Her face lit. "I could be an ornament."

"Or the angel at the top," Slade suggested, parking the car and not quite believing that Taylor and Gracie had convinced him to come along on this trip. The less he had to do with Christmas, the better. "You are quite the angel."

Gracie giggled, then added, "Angels fly and I can't fly. I need a Christmas tree I can climb and hang on a branch 'cause I'm a Gracie ornament."

The logic of a six-year-old had quickly come to fascinate Slade. He grinned at the miniature version of Taylor. His wife. A week ago today they'd gotten married. How crazy was that?

Was it even crazier that he'd convinced her to play along with their marriage for a month? All for the sake of not wanting news of a pending divorce to possibly reach Grandview Pharmaceuticals as it might hurt his chances of landing his dream job and because he didn't want his dad to stress over the holidays. His father had experienced enough rough Christmases over the years. Slade wouldn't be the cause of ruining this one.

Plus, he wanted Taylor so much he couldn't think of anything else but touching her again. Which was proving a little difficult since she kept Gracie between them at all times they weren't at the clinic.

Realizing her argument wasn't working, Gracie changed

tactics. "I bet you'd like to climb a Christmas tree, too, wouldn't you, Mr. Slade?"

Smart kid.

Taylor sent him a warning look.

"Not really. Christmas trees aren't for climbing. But maybe someday soon I'll take you out to my dad's farm in Franklin and we'll find climbing trees."

"Really?" Gracie rubbed her hands together, then climbed out of her car seat and jumped to the ground. "Are there chickens on your farm?"

"No chickens," Slade told her. "But there are horses and cows."

"Princess Vegas has never ridden a horse," Gracie informed him very matter-of-factly. "She thinks she would really like riding a horse. Especially a white one who looks like a unicorn."

"Hmm, I'm not sure if there are any that look like unicorns, but we'll see."

Gracie nodded, then pointed out a family who were also tree shopping. "Look!" She waved at her grinning friend whose face was barely peeking out from beneath her high-collared coat, hat and scarf. "Mommy, can I go say hi to Sarah Beth?"

Sarah Beth, as in the Sarah Beth who was on her soccer team and whose mother screamed and cried a lot?

Waving at a very pregnant woman bundled up in several layers of coats and scarves, Taylor nodded. "That's fine, but walk, don't run."

Doing what could only be called a fast walk, Gracie headed to her friend and hugged her as if it had been months since they'd last seen each other.

Her gaze still on her daughter, Taylor sighed.

Slade stared at her, but she kept her gaze trained on where Gracie and Sarah Beth chatted away, waving their gloved hands around animatedly. "You shouldn't say things to make

Gracie think you're going to be a part of our future. I don't want her hurt."

"Neither do I. But even after we sign divorce papers, there's a ninety-day wait before we go before the judge."

Taylor's attention snapped to him. "You talked to your lawyer today, too, then?"

"Yes. You knew I had a Friday morning appointment, the same as you." He nodded. "He said it'll be after the holidays before anything gets rolling."

Her eyes returned to Gracie. "Mine said the same. Guess it's just as well we didn't open ourselves up for more gossip at work."

He'd spent every evening this week with Taylor and Gracie. They'd eaten, played whatever games Gracie wanted to play, watched cartoons, read her stories and last night they'd pulled boxes out of Taylor's attic and stacked them in the corner of her living room in anticipation of Christmas decorating this weekend.

He could do without the Christmas decorating, but apparently if he wanted to spend time with Taylor, he'd have to endure Christmas festivities. He and his dad had quit celebrating Christmas the year his mom had died. His dad had since started again. His new wife had seen to that. Slade, on the other hand, although not a Scrooge, just didn't see the point.

Each night he'd helped Taylor straighten any mess they'd created, then, while she'd put Gracie to bed, he'd driven home to a house that really wasn't a home at all. Funny how he'd never noticed that before. He'd always liked his uptown condo with all its modern conveniences. Now the place just seemed empty. Good thing he hoped to be moving to New Jersey soon.

Half expecting Taylor to pull away, he grabbed her gloved hand and laced her fingers with his, clasping it tightly as they walked toward Sarah Beth's family. Beneath the fabric he could feel the outline of the wedding ring Taylor still wore. Just as he did beneath his gloves. For their pretend month.

Sarah Beth caught sight of Slade and leaned over to stage-whisper, "Who is he?"

"That's my boyfriend," Gracie informed them, not in a stage whisper. "He's my Prince Charming. When I grow up I'm going to marry him and we're going to live in a magnificent castle and throw grand balls for all our kingdom to enjoy."

Everyone's gazes went to Slade, including a wide-eyed, slightly amused Taylor. Stunned by Gracie's announcement, he cleared his throat.

Laughing, Sarah Beth's mother stuck out her hand. "Hi, I'm Janie. Gracie is my Sarah Beth's best friend. Together they are quite the pair. The entire family will expect an invitation to the wedding, of course. And frequent invitations to visit at the castle."

"I can only imagine." He instantly liked the very pregnant woman, even if she reportedly screamed and cried a lot. Seeing her so pregnant made Slade wonder what Taylor had looked like pregnant with Gracie, what she'd look like if she were pregnant with his child even now from their Vegas weekend. Lord, he hoped she wasn't. He glanced toward her, but she refused to meet his gaze. Her cheeks and nose were already pink from the cold. She was beautiful.

He smiled at Janie. "And, of course, on the castle invitations."

"Janie, this is Slade Sain. He's…" Taylor hesitated and Slade wondered how she would label him. Not husband, not boyfriend, not lover, but who?

"A friend of the family."

Friend of the family? That was accurate up to a point. He was friends with her and Gracie, even if about half the time Taylor treated him more as if he were her enemy. Still, she was cooperating on the pretend month and even smiled at him at work.

"Hoorah for handsome friends, eh, Taylor?" Janie laughed, then, placing a hand on her belly, glanced toward her husband. "We just got here and have to find a tree. My parents are visiting next week and they will be livid if we don't have a tree up for Sarah Beth."

"I hear you. I dread it when my parents visit on Christmas Day."

Real dread showed on her face. Did she not get along with her parents? He'd give anything to have the opportunity to spend time with his parents together again. Then again, maybe her dread had to do with her all-too-real pretend marriage. What had she told her parents?

"We'll let y'all get to it." Taylor glanced around the tree-filled lot. "Hopefully we can find a tree quickly and get in out of this cold."

They went their separate ways. Gracie latched on to Slade's free hand. "Can we put real candy canes on our tree?"

"Sure." After he answered, he realized he should have gotten confirmation from Taylor, but she didn't look upset that he'd answered Gracie's question.

"We could make paper chains to put on it, too."

"If that's what you'd like to do," he agreed.

"It is." Still clinging to his gloved hand, Gracie skipped beside him as if completely unfazed by the cold wind whipping at them. Taylor, on his other side, shivered. In the middle of them, Gracie was holding his one hand and Taylor his other. Warmth spread through Slade's chest. He felt... cozy. He swallowed and fought the feeling down. This was temporary and he was just making the best of a bad situation. It wasn't cozy. Just convenient.

"I think paper chains are beautiful," Gracie continued.

"I'm sure anything you made would be beautiful, princess." Convenient? Could he really lie to himself to that extreme? Spending time with Taylor and Gracie was more than a convenience.

"Mommy always thinks so." Gracie beamed up at him, causing Slade's heart to do a funny chest flop.

Taylor pointed to a blue spruce she spotted a few trees down from them. "It's gorgeous, but it may be too tall. Do you think we can get it inside the house?"

Would it fit through the back double doors of her house?

Slade inspected the tree, thinking that if he'd liked Christmas and had felt the need for a Christmas tree, then Taylor had made a good choice. Perfectly shaped with full branches.

"If not, we could trim some to make it work," he offered. "What do you think, Gracie?"

Gracie eyed the tree and gave him a puzzled look. "How are we gonna fit it inside the van?"

He laughed. Smart, smart kid. "You don't think it'll fit in your seat?"

Gracie giggled. "No way. We could put it on top of Mommy's van. I saw that on a cartoon."

Slade scratched his head. "I'm not sure that's going to work, princess."

"If you don't think we can get it on top of the van, we can pick a smaller tree," Taylor suggested, but her eyes still lingered on the blue spruce.

This was the tree she wanted. The tree he suddenly wanted her to have, even though he saw no logical reason to stuff a tree inside a house and throw glittery decorations on it.

He shook his head. "This is the perfect Christmas tree."

"This Christmas is going to be a perfect Christmas," Taylor mused, almost sounding as if she really believed so.

Not that he'd celebrated Christmas in years, but he was getting sucked into the holiday by a woman so sexy she filled his every waking thought and her six-year-old princess-wannabe daughter, because he wanted to give her that perfect Christmas, to make her holidays filled with joy.

"It is," Gracie agreed, nodding. "Princess Vegas thinks so, too."

"That settles it. Princess Vegas has the best taste." Slade winked at Gracie, got a wink right back that melted him despite the cold wind. "This is our tree. We'll pay and I'll come back later in a truck to pick it up."

"You have a truck?" Taylor looked skeptical. "I can't see you driving a truck."

"No, but my dad does and of course I can drive a truck. I grew up on a farm." Granted he'd spent as much time studying, volunteering and fundraising for breast-cancer awareness as he had hauling hay or herding cattle. But he could do any job on the farm that needed to be done. He loved the land, loved riding his horse and still got a kick out of taking off on a four-wheeler for a carefree afternoon in the country. Nothing like breathing some fresh air and getting up close with nature.

"He lives close?" Taylor still didn't look sure. "We don't want to be a bother. I could call a service and have a tree delivered."

"There's no need to pay inflated prices to a service. My dad's in Franklin. It's about a twenty-minute drive, depending on traffic. I want to do this, Taylor. Let me."

"Of course." Taylor became pensive. "What will you tell him if he asks why you need to borrow a truck?"

"I'll tell him the truth. That I need a truck to pick up a Christmas tree." Or maybe not because wouldn't that cause a slew of questions? His dad knew how he felt about the holidays, and although he and Slade's stepmom both repeatedly invited him over to celebrate the day, he always refused. "Do you want to go to?"

She immediately shook her head. "I don't think that's a good idea. He might…realize the truth."

No doubt both his dad and his stepmom would question

him like crazy regardless. It would be the first time he'd seen them since returning from Vegas. Had he wanted to take Taylor as a way of curtailing their questions?

Glancing down at where Gracie was checking out a cocoon attached to a different tree, Slade whispered back, "You might be right. He does want to meet you, though."

Taylor's brows shot up. Horror paled her face. "Definitely not a good idea."

"I agree. For now."

"This is such a mess." Taylor's lower lip disappeared inside her mouth.

"Only because of Princess here. After you've told her, I think it's a grand idea." He placed his hand on top of Gracie's head and the little girl beamed up at him from beneath the hood of her coat.

"What's a grand idea?"

"Hot chocolate and marshmallows?" he suggested. It wasn't his place to tell her more. Maybe he'd just tell his dad Gracie didn't know because they wanted her to get to know him first. Once they announced their break-up, telling Gracie wouldn't be an issue. Why did the thought of their having to do that bother him so much?

"Mmm-hmm. I'm cold." Gracie wrapped her arms around her body. "Can we go home for hot chocolate?"

"I'll pay for the tree, make sure the guy marks it as sold, then come back with the truck."

"Thank you, but I'll pay for the tree. It would be silly for you to pay for my and Gracie's tree when you'll still have to get one of your own."

"I don't put up a tree, Taylor."

"No Christmas tree?" Gracie piped up, staring at him incredulously. "Are you crazy? What if Santa thinks you don't believe and he doesn't leave you presents? You've got to have a Christmas tree, doesn't he, Mommy?"

"Absolutely. So I'll pay for this one and you help pick out another for his place. We can help decorate it."

Before Slade could argue, Gracie grabbed his hand. "Come on, Mr. Slade, you gotta have a tree for Christmas."

CHAPTER TEN

"SORRY I TOOK so long," Slade told Taylor when she opened the front door much later when he arrived with the tree.

She'd changed from her business clothes into yoga pants and a snowman sweatshirt. Her long blond hair hung in a braid. She'd scrubbed her face clean of the light makeup she'd worn to work that day. Each night was the same. She dressed down. Purposely? To scare him away? He wanted to tell her that it didn't matter what she did. He still wanted her.

"Not a problem." She moved aside so he could enter. "I got your text letting me know you'd been delayed at your dad's."

Closing the front door behind him, Slade frowned. Despite the fact his hands were cold, he grabbed Taylor's warm ones and pulled her gently to him. "Warm me up?"

"Now?" She laughed a little nervously and glanced around her foyer as if seeking an excuse to flee a crime scene.

"Can you think of a better time?"

Her hands trembled within his. "How about never?"

He laughed. "It's hard to believe a week ago I had never met Gracie or held your hand." He squeezed her hand for emphasis. "That I had never kissed you."

"A week ago you had held my hand and kissed me," she corrected, staring at their hands. "As far as Gracie goes, she adores you."

He studied her face, her pensive expression. "Does that bother you? That she likes me?"

She shrugged, making the snowman's hat bell jingle on her shirt. "Should it?"

"No, but I can see that it does." He laced his fingers with hers. "I'm not going to hurt her, Taylor."

She wouldn't meet his eyes. "I hope not."

"Surely you believe I'd never intentionally cause her pain?"

Finally, she lifted her gaze. "I do believe that."

"It's true." He glanced around the foyer and beyond to the living area. "Where is my favorite princess?"

"Asleep. She didn't want to go to bed before you got back but she was fading fast. I promised her we'd get the tree ready to decorate tomorrow." Her expression became pensive again. "I probably shouldn't have promised her that since…"

"Since?"

"Since I shouldn't make plans that include you without your permission. Especially as you don't celebrate Christmas."

He could hear the curiosity in her voice about that, but the last thing he wanted to do was have a conversation with her about his mother's death.

"I'm here, Taylor. Right where I told you I'd be."

"I know."

She refused to look at him again and he'd had enough. He cupped her chin, forcing her gaze upward. "You think I'm going to skip out on the decorating?"

"Tomorrow is Saturday. I'm sure you have other things to do."

"I've rearranged my other obligations for the next month." Normally, he spent his Saturdays with his dad and stepmother, helping out on the farm, unwinding from the week's stressors. All other spare time was spent volunteering with various breast-cancer awareness organizations. "I want to be with you, Taylor."

He wasn't sure he'd ever said truer words. Crazy how a week could change a person's life. He'd always admired her, wanted her, from afar, but now...now she was all he could think about.

"Just because you won it doesn't mean you have to be over here all the time," she clarified. "You shouldn't put off your responsibilities because of me."

He traced his thumb over the smooth lines of her face. "You need to quit trying to back out of giving me my prize."

She met his gaze full on. "You're not getting that prize."

Awareness that they were touching and essentially alone fell over them. Awareness that had her pulling her hands away from his and walking over to where she'd cleared out a corner for the tree.

"I took a pregnancy test at work today. It was negative. I know that's no guarantee and I'll probably do tests weekly until I get my period, but I thought you'd want to know."

"That's good." Because they didn't want her to be pregnant. Emotion hit him. Whether relief or something else, he wasn't sure. Just that strong emotion weighed heavily upon him.

"Yes. The timing was all wrong anyway, but I did the test just to be sure."

He nodded, feeling as if he should say something more but not really knowing what else to say.

"What do you think?" She gestured to the cleared-out corner. "This is where we put our tree last year, but it wasn't nearly as big as the one we picked this evening." She turned questioning eyes on him. Her green gaze searched his, clear, bright, full of sincerity and a good amount of uncertainty, too. "Will it work?"

He'd make it work. He planned to make a lot of things work for the next month.

* * *

"Not there, Mr. Slade. Over here." Gracie directed Slade's top-of-the-tree decorating like a miniprofessional, even framing the tree between her tiny fingers and examining it with one eye closed.

Taylor pulled another ornament out of a box. One that had Gracie's first Christmas photo inside a golden frame. Taylor's heart squeezed. My, how time flew. Not so long ago her little girl had been a precious baby.

"Hey, that's me." Gracie caught sight of what Taylor held and came over for a closer look. "I was so cute."

"And so modest," Taylor mused. She hugged Gracie to her and they both looked at the ornament.

"Not sure modesty comes into play when she's just telling the truth," Slade said, coming down the ladder and checking out what they held. "Hey, you're right. You were cute."

"I was a little baby," Gracie pointed out needlessly. "I was inside Mommy's belly just like Sarah Beth's mommy has a baby." Then she had both adults scrambling for a response. "How did I get inside your belly, Mommy?"

Slade hid a grin and waited to see how Taylor would answer.

"Babies are a special gift and once they are inside a mommy's belly they grow until they are ready to come out into this world."

The look Gracie gave her mother made Slade wonder if the girl would accept the simplified answer. With her schooling, no doubt Gracie knew a lot more about worldly things than Taylor would like. For that matter, probably more than he would like.

He glanced down at her innocent face and felt a protectiveness that made his knees wobble. He'd thought it had been figuratively, but perhaps it had been for real because Taylor and Gracie both stared at him.

"You okay?" Taylor asked.

"Fine."

Only he wasn't. He felt claustrophobic.

He didn't want this. A family. Something he'd not had since his mother had died. Maybe he shouldn't feel that way. He had his father and stepmother, but it just wasn't the same. He was glad his father had found peace. He himself hadn't. Perhaps losing his mother had left him incapable of ever experiencing those bonds again.

He had a purpose, vows he'd made on the day his mother had died, and a wife and kid didn't figure into the equation. Good thing this was only a temporary setup or he might go into a full-blown panic.

"Maybe Mommy should hang the top ornaments." Gracie brought his attention back to the present. "You look drunk."

Determined not to think about the past, or even the future, he stepped down and tickled Gracie's ribs until she pleaded for mercy amidst giggles. "Drunk? What do you know about being drunk?"

Still giggling, she gave him a *duh* expression. "I watch cartoons."

He looked to Taylor for help, but she just gave him a blank look.

"Drunks on cartoons. Who knew?"

"Well, yeah, when the mouse falls into the barrel and comes out all hiccupy and stuff," Gracie clarified very matter-of-factly.

"You think I'm all hiccupy and stuff?" He faked a hiccup for good measure, causing Gracie's eyes to widen and then for her to burst into more giggles.

"Mommy, Mr. Slade is drunk."

He scooped Gracie into his arms and twirled her around. "If I spin enough, we'll both be drunk."

Gracie begged for more when he stopped.

"You don't know what you've started," Taylor warned, watching them with an expression he couldn't quite read. And not because his brain had yet to catch up with his spinning body.

"Gracie, with you around I wouldn't need to go to the gym." Slade collapsed onto the sofa next to Taylor.

Gracie crawled into his lap and flattened her palms against his cheeks. "More. More."

"You've tuckered him out," Taylor informed her daughter. "He's old and needs his rest. Besides, you need to finish hanging your ornaments."

"I don't want to."

"Gracie."

Gracie's chin dropped so low it almost dragged on the floor. She cut her gaze to Slade. "Maybe we could spin more after I hang the rest of my ornaments?"

"Slade may have other things he needs to do today beside help you hang ornaments."

"Do you?" Gracie pinned him on the spot.

He shook his head. "Despite being old and needing my rest—" he gave a pointed look at Taylor "—I'm yours all day, princess."

"I'm glad." Gracie wrapped her arms around him and squeezed tight.

"Me, too, princess." He soaked up the goodness of her hug and ignored the panic threatening to resurface. "Me, too."

Taylor and Gracie eyed their finished product. A fully decorated Christmas tree with twinkling colorful lights.

"It looks magical," Gracie breathed.

They'd decorated the tree before Slade had left to take his dad's truck back, but had just finished decorating the rest of the room with garlands and bows and pretty knickknacks. During that time daylight had disappeared and they'd just clicked the remote to turn on all the Christmas lights in the room.

Taylor glanced at her daughter. Gracie stared at the tree with wide eyes and awe. Through the eyes of a child. Nothing had ever seemed so magical as the wonder reflected on her baby girl's face.

"You're right," she agreed. "It does look magical."

"Just wait until Mr. Slade sees it. He's gonna love it."

Slade had said he'd come back. That had been a few hours ago. It was now early evening. On a Saturday. Despite what he'd said, no doubt he would have more exciting things to do. Why would he keep hanging around when she would barely even kiss him, much less all the other things he wanted from her?

How she was holding out she didn't know. It sure wasn't that she didn't want him. With each passing day the need within her grew more ferocious. She couldn't give in. To give in would only further complicate their situation. At least on her part. She couldn't have sex with Slade and not get emotionally attached.

But wasn't that happening with spending time with him? With watching him with her daughter? Sure, he was awkward at times, but overall the man had Gracie wrapped around his finger. Or was it the other way around?

"I think you're right," she agreed with Gracie. "How could anyone not love such a magical tree?"

The song playing on the Christmas station they were listening to changed and "Rockin' Around the Christmas Tree" came on. They looked at each other. Taylor cranked the volume up several notches. Grabbing each other's hands, they began to shimmy and shake and rock in front of their Christmas tree.

Happiness filled Taylor at her daughter's laughter. The song was their Christmas favorite and one that they always stopped what they were doing and danced to. She couldn't remember when they'd started the tradition. Probably when Gracie had been two, although perhaps it had been three.

Taylor treasured those happy, silly, giggly times.

They bounced around, twisting their tushes, laughing, slinging their arms around.

"I guess you didn't hear when I knocked," Slade said, leaning against the living room door frame. "Now I see why."

Mortified that he'd seen her shaking and shimmying, Taylor felt her giddiness evaporate and she stopped moving.

Or tried to.

Gracie grabbed her hand and waved her arms as she continued to dance with all her little heart. "Come join us, Mr. Slade. We're doing the Christmas rock, Mommy-and-Gracie style. We rule."

Unable to resist her daughter's enthusiasm, Taylor began a somewhat modified version of her earlier dancing. There was nothing stylish about the way she was twisting, but she refused to let Slade ruin their fun.

She met his blue gaze, daring him to make fun of her. She wasn't quite sure what she'd do if he did, but she'd figure that out on an as-needed basis.

His eyes twinkled with mischief, but he didn't comment on her dancing skills—or lack thereof. "I'll just watch the show."

She arched a brow. "Chicken?"

About time she turned his teasing around on him.

"Come on, Mr. Slade." Gracie bounced to the beat of the music. "It's fun."

"Yeah, Mr. Slade, come on. It's fun," Taylor taunted, crooking her finger and enjoying herself more than she'd have believed possible when she'd spotted him.

Slade pushed off the door frame and strolled toward them. Strolled because walk didn't begin to describe the swagger to his gait as he crossed over to them.

"Okay, but just remember you two asked for this and I did try to spare you." His gaze locked with Taylor's, he joined in, taking one of Gracie's hands and one of Taylor's, and began moving.

Heat spread up her arm at the feel of his skin against hers. He squeezed her hand, smiled, and Taylor couldn't keep from smiling back. Darn him. She didn't want to like him or enjoy that he was touching her or to share her Mommy-and-Gracie Christmas dance with him.

Only she was and it felt so right. All of it. Everything about him.

It had only been a week and already she was weakening in ways that went beyond the tingles attacking her senses. What was she going to feel like at the end of their month? If only she didn't know he was a player, and once a player always a player. Men might be able to change for a short while, but ultimately they always went back to playing.

It's what had happened with Kyle. It's what would happen with Slade.

He'd even said as much. He wasn't promising ever after or anything more than a monthlong affair.

The song ended, but another upbeat song about a Spanish Christmas came on. Gracie let go of their hands and began wholeheartedly singing along with the words she knew.

Taylor seized the opportunity to pull her hand free from Slade's and to step away.

"Taylor?"

Feeling choked, she shook her head and walked over to a stack of plastic bins. She fiddled with the empty boxes and bags inside, rearranging items, then closing the lid.

"Taylor?" he repeated.

"Don't you have somewhere you need to be?" she snapped, hating it that her eyes watered.

"Mr. Slade, did you see the tree?" Gracie interrupted, tugging on his hand and demanding his attention.

"Yes, when I was dancing I saw the tree. You and your mom did an amazing job."

"We did. You, too."

"I only put stuff where you told me to," he reminded her.

"That's still helping, right, Mommy?"

"Right," she agreed, grateful for Gracie's interruption so she could regain her composure.

"Are you two fabulous Christmas decorators hungry?"

Gracie nodded. "Famished." She dramatically put her hands across her belly.

"Can I take you somewhere?"

"Pippa's Pizza Palace?" Gracie piped up.

"Probably not again this soon," Taylor said, thinking she couldn't stomach greasy pizza tonight.

"She's just saying that because she knows I'll beat her at Skee-Ball again."

"Sure. That's the reason I don't want to eat overpriced mediocre pizza again this soon," she assured.

"It wasn't that bad."

"It wasn't that good either," she reminded him.

Although his gaze still searched her face, Slade laughed. "So, what's another restaurant Gracie likes?"

Gracie yelled out the name of her favorite Japanese hibachi grill.

Slade's brow rose. "You like sushi?"

"She'll eat it, but she's more into the steak and the show."

"Kid after my own heart. Hibachi it is."

Three weeks had passed since Taylor had married Slade. Three weeks in which her pregnancy tests had remained negative and she'd spent an inordinate amount of time with him. He really had set aside whatever his other obligations were because he spent every moment he wasn't at work with her and Gracie.

"It's only five more days until Christmas," Slade pointed out to the little girl in his lap.

Five days. Then her month with Slade would soon be over and then…and then what? He'd wanted the month so he could actively pursue having an affair with her. The sexual chemistry was always there, burning just below the surface, simmering and threatening to rise to a boil, but other than light touches that sent her nerves into overdrive, lingering looks that made her want to both run and hide, and strip him naked, and his lightly flirtatious comments, he hadn't pushed. Why not? She was so on edge she almost wanted him to push just so she could get angry at him.

She glanced at the other end of the sofa where Gracie was curled up in his lap. They were studying a department-store sales flyer as if it contained all the secrets to the world.

"I think Princess Vegas might like this one best." Gracie pointed to an item on a particular page.

"You think?" Slade studied the page with all serious-ness. "I don't know. Princess Vegas might think getting a kitchen set to be insulting. After all, princesses don't cook."

"Princesses can cook if they want to cook," Gracie edu-cated him. "Princesses just don't have to cook if they don't want to cook. Someone else has to do the dishes. Princesses never do the dishes."

"Unless they want to," Slade added, to which Gracie frowned and Taylor fought a smile.

"Gracie, I'm not sure that toy kitchen set will fit in Santa's sleigh."

"It will. Santa's sleigh is magic. If it can fly, it can hold all the toys for good boys and girls. Besides, some people get ponies and stuff. How do you think they all fit?" She paused for effect. "Magic."

"She makes a good argument." Slade looked as if he was fighting back a smile.

Taylor nodded. Her daughter was pretty sharp. "Well, let's hope you've been a very good girl this year, then, so Santa can bring you that."

"The kitchen is for Princess Vegas, but I have been a very good girl, Mommy."

"I think you have, but who knows what Santa's been told?" Taylor teased.

Gracie thought about that a few seconds. "Sarah Beth is getting her picture taken with Santa tomorrow at the mall. I should go and make sure Santa knows I've been a good girl."

"I think you should." Slade glanced toward Taylor.

"What do you think, Mom? You up for a trip to the mall tomorrow?"

"No parking places, crowded stores, long lines waiting to see Santa? Bring it on," she agreed. How could she not at the image of Gracie and Slade on the sofa, both looking so expectantly at her?

Slade laughed. "You've obviously done this before."

"A few times."

"You two will have to humor me. I've never done the Santa-at-the-mall thing."

Taylor frowned. So he didn't have kids and didn't want kids, but what about when he had been a kid? "Where did you grow up? Siberia?"

"Here, in Nashville."

"Then how did you avoid Santa at the mall?"

"I may have been when I was really small but, if so, I don't remember. My mom got sick when I was pretty young and we just didn't do that kind of thing."

"What kind of sickness?" Gracie rubbed his cheek in what Taylor assumed was her way of trying to comfort Slade.

"Breast cancer." His eyes were focused on the flyer he and Gracie still held.

Taylor's gaze stayed fixed on him and her hands wanted to rub his cheek, too, if it would give any comfort to the raw ache she'd heard in his two words. "Breast cancer?"

"Yes."

His mother had died of breast cancer and now he was an oncologist? Coincidence? Taylor doubted it. "How old were you?"

"When Mom was first diagnosed? Five. I was twelve when she died. She put up a great fight."

"I'm sorry."

"Me, too."

"Me, too," Gracie added, just to remind them that although she hadn't been saying much she'd been taking in their conversation.

Slade pulled her to him, kissed the top of her head, then changed the subject. "So, what do you think Santa needs to bring for your mom?"

Gracie put her finger to the side of her mouth and looked thoughtful, then scooted farther up in his lap and whispered in his ear. She glanced toward Taylor and giggled, then said something else.

Slade's eyes got big. "Seriously?"

Gracie nodded. "It's what she really wants."

"Interesting." Slade gave Taylor a look that made her feel nervous. "Does Santa do that?"

A puzzled look came over Gracie's face and then she shrugged. "He's magic, remember?"

Curious, Taylor crossed her arms. "What are you two up to?"

Gracie giggled. "Plotting your Christmas present."

"She put in a pretty tall request, but since it's what you really want…"

"I guess I'll find out in five days if I've been good or bad this year."

"Or maybe you've been really good at being bad?"

Gracie giggled. Taylor arched a brow.

"I'm pretty sure Santa is going to leave a bunch of coal in your stocking, Slade Sain." She paused. "Did you ever get your tree decorated?"

He shook his head. "It's in my living room, but that's it. I'm not much on Christmas decorations."

"Gracie and I should help you decorate." Maybe it was how his voice had cracked, how he'd tried to look so un-affected when he'd said his mother had had breast can-cer, but Taylor wanted to do something for him. Goodness knew, he'd done enough for her and Gracie over the past few weeks.

"I'd like that."

"Then that's what we'll plan to do tomorrow after we go to the mall."

"That'll work because I'll have to pick up some orna- ments and the like while we're there."

"You don't have ornaments?" Gracie sounded stunned. "How old are you?"

He shook his head. "We won't talk about how old I am but, no, I don't have any ornaments."

"I should make you some," Gracie offered.

"I'd like that."

Taylor would swear that his voice broke and that his eyes glistened more than a little.

Gracie climbed out of his lap and headed to her room.

"She is a wonderful kid, Taylor."

"I think so." Needing to be closer to him, to bring a smile back to his face, Taylor scooted near to where he sat. "What was Gracie's suggestion for my Christmas present?"

Looking grateful for the distraction from how emo- tional he'd gotten moments before, he shook his head. "Ask Gracie."

"I'm asking you."

"I'm not telling."

"Why not?"

"Because it's for me to know and for you to find out."

"That is so childish."

"Guilty as charged."

She picked up a sofa pillow and tossed it at him.

He caught it. "You wanna play?"

"Not really," she denied, but her gaze stayed locked with his mischievous one. She much preferred this look to the sad one that had taken hold in his eyes.

"Then you shouldn't have started something you didn't want to finish." He scooted closer, the pillow in his hands.

"Don't do it."

"Or what?"

"Or…or…" She couldn't think of any threat that even

halfway made sense, so she grabbed another pillow, whacked him over the head and shot off the sofa.

He caught her before she'd taken two steps, pulling her down into his lap. "Naughty, naughty, Taylor. Don't you know Santa is watching?"

"Santa isn't real," she told him, twisting halfheartedly to free herself from his hold, but his arms tightened around her.

"Don't you let my girl hear you say that."

"She's my girl, and I'd never say that in front of Gracie. I want her to believe in all things good."

Was he staring at her mouth? Because she really thought he was staring at her mouth.

She held her breath.

He was definitely staring at her mouth. "I want to kiss you, Taylor, but Gracie is just in her room."

"I know." She did know.

"Do you want me to kiss you?"

"I'm not going to answer that."

"Because you do?"

"I'm not going to answer that either."

He laughed.

Taylor didn't. Because she wanted him to kiss her. They'd been married for three weeks. Three weeks. They were getting divorced.

Yet she couldn't imagine her life without him.

Which really wasn't good because she didn't want to become dependent on him.

She started to rise from his lap, but he hugged her to him. "Don't go."

"I have things to do," she argued, needing to get away from him so she could clear her head. "I need to check on Gracie."

"We'll both go."

He made everything sound so good, as if life was full of possibilities, as if they could make this work. Then again, she'd believed Kyle when he'd convinced her of that, too.

CHAPTER ELEVEN

KYLE WOULD HAVE been cursing before they'd even pulled into the mall parking lot. Taylor's father would have made one loop, declared the whole thing a disaster and told her there was no Santa but that he'd buy her one item off her list so to choose wisely.

However, Slade dropped Taylor and Gracie off at the front entrance so they could secure a place in line to see Santa. Then, still whistling a tune, he drove off in her minivan to search out a most likely nonexistent parking space.

Twenty minutes after letting them out at the front mall entrance, Slade joined them in the Santa line.

"You're just in time," Gracie told him excitedly. "It's almost my turn."

"Glad I didn't miss it. I wanted to see you with Santa."

"Sorry this is so much trouble," Taylor apologized.

Slade just shrugged. "This isn't that much trouble. Besides, if it makes her smile and you smile, it's worth a whole lot more than the effort to find a parking space."

"How come you're so nice?"

"Because I know what's beneath your clothes and I want another peek." He waggled his brows.

Taylor's eyes widened, surprised at his reply and a little flattered, too, even though she said, "Typical male response."

"I am a man."

"So all this is about sex?" she whispered, for his ears only. "Because you haven't even kissed me."

And maybe because she didn't quite believe that his answer hadn't been a cover because he hadn't wanted to tell her why he was really so nice to her and Gracie.

His eyes searched hers. "Have you wanted me to kiss you, Taylor? I asked you last night and you wouldn't answer. If you'll recall, our agreement was that I'd only do what you wanted me to do. I want you. I've been blunt about that. What do you want?"

She was saved from answering by Gracie excitedly tugging on her hand. "I'm next."

Fortunately, her daughter's full attention was all on the Santa and, unfortunately, Slade hadn't been distracted at all.

"Well?"

She shook her head. Discussing this in line to see Santa wasn't the right time or place. "It doesn't matter."

"It does."

"I was just making a point that if all this is about sex, then it doesn't make sense that you haven't, well, you know, pushed for sex."

Slade smiled and looked so smug that you'd think it was him next in line with Santa. "You've been thinking about Vegas."

"It's my turn!" Gracie grabbed their attention. "Mommy, take my picture."

"Actually, you can't," an elf informed them. "Picture packages with Santa are available for a small fee." He pointed his finger to a table on the other side of the line. "When she finishes with Santa, just head over there and they'll fix you up with all the pictures you want."

Taylor and Slade watched Gracie whisper a long request to Santa, for Santa to look their way, then her to nod and say more. The Santa looked an awful lot like the Santa who had married them in Vegas, but, then, they were both impersonating a jolly old man wearing red and having a snowy-white beard. For that matter, the elf kind of reminded her of the limo driver…but that was crazy.

She shook her head, thinking Slade's comment about Vegas must have put the notion in her mind.

"There's no telling what she's asking for," she mused, mostly to make sure the subject didn't go back to sex…or the lack thereof.

"You think she's changed her mind from the toy kitchen?"

Still studying the Santa and his elf helpers, wondering at the resemblance to the Vegas Santa and his helpers, Taylor shrugged. "Kids tend to change their minds a dozen times before Christmas actually arrives."

"I hope not."

Something in the way he said it made Taylor look at him more closely. "Why?"

He grinned. "Because this Santa went online and ordered a certain toy kitchen set."

"What if I've already bought that for her?"

"Then I will cancel my order," he immediately offered, not looking upset in the slightest.

Again, a very different response than her father or Kyle would have had if she'd done something that had messed with their plans. She knew she shouldn't compare Slade to them, but she couldn't seem to help herself.

"Have you?" he prompted.

"I haven't, but you didn't need to buy her such a big item."

"I'll keep that in mind when I buy your present." His eyes twinkled.

Heat warmed her insides. He planned to buy her a gift? Why did that mean so much more than it should? "I know you don't celebrate the holidays, so don't bother getting me a present."

"There's one to me under your tree. Gracie had me shake it and try to figure out what it was."

So maybe he was just getting her a gift in response to her gift. Still, it was the thought that counted and for a man who claimed not to celebrate Christmas to make the effort did funny things to her insides.

"It's just a little something."

"I'll get you a little something, too," he promised.

"Did you see me with Santa?" Happiness shone in Gracie's eyes. "He said I had been a very good girl and that I was going to get all kinds of presents this year."

"He did?" Taylor shot a concerned look toward Santa. Man, he looked a lot like Vegas Santa. But no way could it be the same guy. The dude really shouldn't build up kids' expectations so high. A lot of parents would do well to buy one or two of the items on their kids' lists.

"Yep, he said you were going to get what you wanted for Christmas this year, too. That he's sorry about last year, but you never said anything until Christmas Day and then it was too late."

"He did?" she repeated, yet again looking at the Santa. The man's attention had already turned to the next kid climbing into his lap, but he glanced up and winked at Taylor.

What? Taylor stared in slight disbelief at the resemblance, telling herself to stop being silly and to pay attention to her daughter.

Gracie showed them the little stocking filled with a few pieces of candy that Santa had given her and then they were ushered over to the photo table where a computer screen had pictures of Gracie with Santa pulled up.

They couldn't decide which of the three shots they liked best, so Taylor ended up buying two of them and Slade bought the other because he thought it might have been his favorite and he couldn't leave the print behind.

They shopped for a few gifts Taylor still hadn't picked up, Gracie helping to decide between several items for Nina, then they drove to her favorite hibachi grill.

By the time they got to Slade's house, had the small tree decorated with the ornaments Gracie had made him with construction paper, glitter and glue, and a string of colorful lights, Gracie was tired and curled up on his sofa to watch a movie on television. In less than five minutes she was asleep.

"I guess we should be going," Taylor said, feeling awkward in his condo now that Gracie was out like a light.

"We were so busy decorating my poor little tree that you never saw the rest of the condo. Let me show you."

"Okay," she agreed, not knowing what else to say.

His place was beautiful, airy, spacious and clean. No toys or little handprints anywhere. Everything modern, high-tech and looking like it should be featured in a magazine article on the perfect bachelor pad.

They came to his bedroom. She refused to look at the bed. Then they went into his bathroom and he had an amazing rain shower and tub. Flashbacks to that last morning in Vegas and the shower they'd shared had her face heating. Oh, my.

"That is seriously cool." She eyed the tub and tried to keep her mind off Vegas. "Gracie could swim in it."

They both stared at the tub. "It's a shame I don't use it more often."

"Just let me know when and I'll come make use of it for you." Ugh. Had she really just said that? She hadn't meant… Or maybe she had. What was wrong with her? Thoughts of Vegas? Part of her wished she could blink her eyes and they would be back to that weekend away from reality.

"Anytime, Taylor."

His voice changed, taking on a raspy quality, and her gaze lifted to his. He watched her with awareness, hot and heavy, as if his mind was filled with the image of her in his tub, of them in his tub. Was he thinking about Vegas?

Her heart rate kicked up. "Sorry, I didn't mean…"

"Taylor?"

"Mmm?"

"Shh." He grabbed her wrist and pulled her to him.

Her cheek pressed up against his chest. The material of

his shirt was soft, smelled of him, made her want to snuggle in closer to the sound of his heartbeat.

His fingers were in the pulled-up tangles of her hair. His lips were brushing the top of her head. His thumbs caressed her face.

"I know Gracie is asleep in the living room, but I need to touch you, Taylor. Even if just a little. Tell me that's what you want, too."

She knew what he meant. Being pressed against him felt so good. But she couldn't forget Gracie was just a few rooms away and could wake anytime.

He gently sucked against her nape.

Taylor almost moaned. Okay, so she did moan, the sound jarring her back to reality. She bit the inside of her lip.

"I know what you say you want," he continued, his eyes flickering with emotion. "When we touch, when you look at me, your body says something completely different."

She willed her body to silence. "We both know you are an attractive, skilled man. Of course I respond to you. It doesn't mean anything."

"So if we kiss and touch, it's nothing more than appeasing our sexual appetites?" he elaborated, moving even closer to her.

"Right." Had her voice cracked?

"Which means there's no reason why we shouldn't kiss, why we shouldn't give each other pleasure, because we both know the score."

"Right." That time she knew her voice had cracked.

He spun her so she was facing herself in the mirror that ran the entire length of the massive sink and countertop. He moved close so that his body pressed against hers, so that his hardness pressed into the softness of her backside. Taylor gulped.

He shifted against her. Excited shivers shot through her body. He kissed her, thoroughly, completely, making her practically gasp for air. His hands traveled over her body, leaving a wake of awareness, of need.

"None of this matters because a few months from now it will all be as if we never happened," he continued. "We'll go on with our lives just as if Vegas never happened."

Her gaze searched his in the mirror. She was reminded of the night he'd made love to her in Vegas, when he'd stripped her in front of the mirror. He'd been full of tenderness and passion. Now his eyes burned with something different, something she couldn't quite label.

Something that made her long for things she knew better than to long for. She wouldn't be able to forget him, wouldn't be able to think of Christmas without thinking of him, of their wedding ceremony performed by Santa, of his decorating with her and Gracie, of how wonderful the past few weeks had been with him at her side.

Because he made her want to believe in the magic of the holidays, that dreams could come true, even crazy ones that seemed almost impossible, such as a playboy changing into a Prince Charming. Her Prince Charming.

Only he wasn't and that was like a bucket of cold water over her head.

"You and I did happen, Slade, and that changed everything," she admitted, so softly she was surprised he could make out her words. He must have, though, because rather than resume kissing her, as she'd expected, as she'd longed for, panted for, he stepped back, turned from her, and walked out of the bathroom with a growled comment about going to check on Gracie.

"Ho-ho-ho, merry Christmas!" Slade called out as he pushed the front door to Taylor's house closed. A house that felt more and more like home to him. Which was why he needed to forget having an affair with Taylor, see her and Gracie past the holidays, then push them from his mind.

In two days he'd be flying to Newark to tour Grandview Pharmaceuticals and negotiate the offer for his dream job.

The call had come the day before and although he'd been over the moon, he'd found himself unable to tell anyone other than his father. His father, who had asked yet again when Slade was going to bring his new family to the farm for a visit and what they thought of moving to Newark. He had hummed and hawed enough to let his dad know that what Taylor and Gracie thought really wasn't a deciding factor in his decision.

They weren't.

This was the opportunity he'd dreamed of, the perfect smokescreen for Taylor and him to quietly divorce without any holiday or life drama for either of them, without Grandview bigwigs discovering that their new clinical research director had married and planned a divorce the same weekend. A win all the way around.

"Mr. Slade!" Gracie almost toppled him over as she launched herself at him, hugging him tightly.

Forgetting Taylor and Gracie wasn't going to be easy. She'd been right when she'd said they had happened and it had changed everything. Only he refused to let it change everything. He knew what he wanted, what his life goals were, and nothing was going to stand in the way of that.

Nothing and no one. He'd enjoy his time left with them, then he'd leave and not look back.

"Hey, princess." He set the packages he held on to the wooden foyer floor and hugged the little girl to him, loving the warmth and genuineness to her embrace. "You ready for Santa Claus to come tonight?"

Gracie nodded. "It's going to be amazing."

"That good this year, eh?"

Blond curls bounced up and down again. "Do you want a cookie? Mommy and I have been baking them for Santa."

Slade caught sight of Taylor standing in the doorway, watching them. As usual, she stole his breath.

His wife. But not for much longer. Soon he'd pack his belongings and move to another state, live the life he'd always wanted. A life where he focused on finding a cure for a disease that had robbed him of so much. That had robbed so many of so much. He had no regrets.

"Hey," she greeted him, a bit breathy sounding herself.

"Hey, yourself." He soaked in every bit of her. From her caught-up-in-a-ponytail hair, to the Christmas sweater and yoga pants, to her washed-clean face. He was leaving in two days. The thought made him want to grab her, throw her over his shoulder and lock them in her bedroom for the remainder of the time they had left.

"Come on, Mr. Slade. Come see the cookies we made. I put icing on them and sparkling things you can eat." Gracie tugged on his hand, reminding him of why he wouldn't be doing any of the things he longed to do with Taylor.

"Help me carry these to the tree." He motioned to the brightly wrapped cartoon-princess-covered packages. "Then lead me to the cookies."

Gracie giggled and began inspecting the presents. "Are these all for me?" she asked, big eyed.

He nodded. He'd gone overboard, but he'd never had a kid to buy for in the past, never would in the future and he wanted Gracie's Christmas to be special. It would be the only one he shared with her.

The thought of missing her future Christmases, of missing her, shot sadness through him. Which was ridiculous. He was getting what he wanted. He should be over the moon.

Gracie smiled at him. "That's a lot of presents."

Fingering a dangling blond curl because he needed to touch her, he pointed out, "You did say you'd been a really good girl this year."

She nodded, grabbed up a package and took off toward the living room where the tree was.

"You didn't have to get her so much."

"I had fun shopping for her." True. Even though it had

been years since he'd bought more than a gift card, he had enjoyed searching out gifts for Gracie.

"I can see you now in the little-girl section of the toy store," Taylor teased.

Slade took her hand, pulled her to him for a brief kiss to the cheek. "You smell good." He breathed in the scent of her hair.

"Like cookies?" She didn't pull away. Which surprised him. Thrilled him. Made him wonder what else he could do that she wouldn't pull away from.

"Like you."

"Flatterer."

"It's the truth."

"Do you always tell the truth, Slade?"

Her question seemed an odd one. Did she know about Grandview? Was she testing him to see if he'd tell her? Or was that his guilty conscience because she didn't know? He would tell her. Tonight. He studied her expression, then shrugged. "I try to be honest."

"It's a good policy. Prevents confusion down the road."

"Yeah." If she knew he was leaving, why didn't she just say so? Then again, how could she? He'd just found out the day before.

The timer on the oven dinged.

"Time to take out the last batch. You want to help decorate? The other batches should be cool by now."

He soaked in her smile, the warmth of her expression, and wondered how many nights he'd spend thinking about her in Newark. He suspected too many.

"Sure," he agreed. "But I have to warn you, I'm more of an expert cookie eater than decorator."

"Will you read me another good-night story?" Gracie yawned and stretched out in her bed. "I'm not sleepy."

"I can see that," Taylor agreed, smiling down at her

daughter. "I guess we can do one more story, since it's Christmas Eve and all."

Gracie turned big green eyes on Slade, who stood in the doorway. "Will you lie down next to me and listen, too?"

"Gracie—" Taylor began, but Slade dismissed her concerns.

"Sure."

Despite his looking a little uncomfortable, he lay next to Gracie and she snuggled into the crook of his arm, grinning up at him. "Mommy is a very good storyteller."

His expression difficult to assess, he answered, "I've heard."

"I'm not sure about that, but I can read a book." They'd just finished *The Night Before Christmas*, so Taylor reached for one of Gracie's all-time favorites about a mischievous little girl with an active imagination.

Gracie looked up at Slade. "You're going to love this. It's so good."

Taylor began to read. Occasionally, Gracie would giggle and poke Slade. "See," she'd say.

Taylor kept reading until Gracie's eyes closed, then she finished the chapter and closed the book.

She stared at the image of Gracie tucked against Slade and her heart melted. That's how it was supposed to be, she thought. How it should be.

Her gaze shifted to his and so many emotions shot through her. Mostly emotions of longing. Not just for the physical things he did to her body but for the way he'd turned her and Gracie's lives upside down over the past weeks. She had one week left with him. Then what? They told the world they'd made a mistake and were divorcing? Would he still be a part of their lives or would he go back to how things had been before Vegas?

She set the book back on Gracie's shelf and began untangling her daughter from Slade.

"I love you, Mommy," Gracie mumbled, not really awake.

"I love you, too, sweetheart."

"I love you, too, Mr. Slade."

Taylor's gaze went to Slade's. He stared at the sleeping little girl, but didn't respond other than to lose color from his face.

She might be getting all soft and mushy on the inside, but Slade wasn't. She'd do well to remember that.

Her throat constricting, Taylor moved away from the bed and left the room. She went into the kitchen and began unloading the dishwasher. He hadn't said the words back to Gracie. Because they weren't true? Because he'd told her earlier that he tried to always be honest?

Yes, she was biased, but how could he not have fallen for the little girl as much as Gracie had fallen for him? Right or wrong, she believed he had. So why hadn't he been able to admit it?

"Do you know if you're pregnant?"

Not having heard him come into the kitchen, she jumped, startled at his presence as much as at his words. Gracie's sleepy declaration had made him wonder if Taylor was pregnant. She paused midway to the cabinet, cup in hand. "I'm not."

"You're sure?" His voice was rough. Rougher than it should be, asking such a sensitive question. Or maybe she was just being too sensitive because she'd cried when she'd started her period. Tears of relief and tears of loss. How crazy was that?

"I'm sure. I told you I wasn't after the last negative pregnancy test, and I finished my period yesterday so I know I'm not. I guess I should have told you about getting my period, too."

He nodded as if that's what he'd expected her to say. "I thought you had. You drank coffee at work this week."

The man was observant. She'd give him that. "That made you think I wasn't pregnant?"

"Despite your negative pregnancy tests, you'd not had a cup since Vegas."

Yep, he was too observant for his own good.

"I started vitamins and stopped my bad habits just in case, but nothing came of Vegas."

Nothing came of Vegas. The words ripped at her heart. What had she wanted to come of Vegas? Nothing. Nothing at all because she'd never planned for Vegas to happen.

"I'm glad," he told her. "A pregnancy would have made everything more difficult."

Taylor gulped back the stab of pain she shouldn't be feeling. "You're right."

Because they were temporary, were getting a divorce, were only together to keep from having so much life turmoil with family and at work right before the holidays. Yet she'd not met his father or stepmother. Since Slade claimed not to celebrate the holidays, she supposed it made sense, but he'd not even mentioned her and Gracie meeting his family since the night they'd bought the Christmas trees.

Why didn't he celebrate Christmas?

She put a cup in the cabinet, shut the door and dared him to look away from her. After his not responding to Gracie, she just dared him to ignore her. "Tell me about your mother."

His face paled almost as much as it had when Gracie had told him she loved him. "My mother? Why?"

Why? Good question when they were only pretending. Only was she really? Would his comment about her being pregnant have hurt so much if she was only pretending?

"I want to understand you," she admitted. She wanted to understand why he changed relationships so often, why he felt the way he did about marriage and kids, to understand why he'd not said three simple words back to a child he obviously adored.

"There really isn't a point, is there?"

Exactly what she'd just thought, but she couldn't let it go.

"It's Christmas Eve. Humor me."

He raked his fingers through his hair. "Let's go sit in the living room. I'll tell you, but it's really not that interesting a story."

For a not so interesting story, they talked until almost midnight. Once he started talking he couldn't seem to quit. Maybe to distract himself from the panic that had gripped him when Gracie had told him she loved him. Maybe because he'd almost said the words back. But he couldn't love the little girl. Sure, he cared about her and Taylor, but he didn't love them. So instead of analyzing all the unwelcome emotions that had taken hold of him he told Taylor about when he'd first realized his mother was sick, her frequent trips in and out of the hospital, about the sticky notes she'd write him every day.

"That's why you give your patients those notes?"

He nodded. "It just feels right, like I'm keeping a part of her alive."

"You keep her alive just by being you."

Talking about his mother helped, reminded him of his life goals, grounding him to the future he'd chosen. "She was a special lady."

"I wish I could have met her."

He pulled out his wallet and withdrew a photo. It was a family shot of him, his dad, and his mother. Slade had been about five at the time.

She'd been upset when they'd started talking, but her attitude had softened long ago. "You look a lot like her."

"Thank you."

Taylor studied the picture. "How old was she when she died?"

"Thirty-three." The words tore from his heart.

Taylor grimaced. "That's so young."

He nodded. "Too young to have dealt with the things she dealt with." He stared at the photo, lots of old memories slamming him. Good, he needed those memories to keep his mind on track. He slid the picture back into his wallet, wondering why he'd let Taylor convince him to talk about his mother. Then again, maybe he'd told her because it was the perfect lead in to telling her that he was leaving, that he was taking a job to fulfill the vow he'd made in his mother's memory. Definitely he'd wanted a distraction from Gracie's sleepy words and their shattering effect.

"You were too young to have dealt with the things you dealt with, too," Taylor mused, taking his hand. "I'm sorry."

His heart squeezed and he didn't like the jitteriness shooting through his veins. Neither did he want her pity. "It's okay."

"Not really, but I understand what you mean."

They sat there, holding hands and staring at the Christmas tree for long moments, each lost in their own thoughts. He knew where his mind was, where he needed their conversation to go, but instead they sat in silence. Finally, Taylor stood.

"I guess it's time for Santa to show."

Slade arched a brow at her. "Santa?"

"You know what I mean and, no, I'm not putting a red suit and beard on."

The image of Taylor dressed as Santa had a real smile tugging at his lips. "Too bad. You'd rock a red suit and wig."

"Maybe, but Gracie will be just as happy with Santa arriving and eating his cookies sans a wig and red suit."

"I could help take care of those cookies for you," he offered, wiggling his brows and wondering why he wasn't redirecting their conversation to Grandview.

"Have at them. She also left a glass of milk, but since it's been out of the fridge a few hours I'd recommend tossing it rather than drinking it."

Taylor disappeared into her bedroom and came back carrying some plastic bags. Wondering at himself, at his reluctance to bring up a subject that he suspected would ruin their remaining time together, Slade made haste with the cookies while she pulled out stocking stuffers and gifts from the bags.

"She's going to be so excited when she wakes up."

"I wish I could see her," he murmured, not realizing he'd said the words out loud until Taylor's head spun toward him. How much he meant the words surprised him. He really would like to be there when Gracie woke, when she stumbled half-asleep into the living room and saw her gifts.

But not because he loved the little girl. Just that he'd spent so much time with Taylor and Gracie over the past few weeks that of course he wanted to be there when she experienced Christmas morning.

He watched Taylor consider offering to let him stay. His lungs didn't seem to be working correctly. He wanted to stay, to make love to Taylor, to wake up next to her, and experience Christmas morning with her and Gracie. Part of him wanted to take her into his arms and seduce her into letting him stay. Another part had his lungs constricting so tightly he had to go.

He couldn't stay, couldn't complicate the fact he was leaving the day after Christmas by having sex with Taylor when he suspected doing so would make leaving more difficult. For them both.

"What time is too early for me to arrive?"

"It's Christmas. She'll probably be up at the crack of dawn." She met his gaze. "It's already very late. You won't get but a few hours' sleep at most. Maybe you should stay?"

"I'll be fine heading home. I can sleep when I'm old." Or when he was in Newark. Alone.

Fulfilling his lifelong dream.

Disappointment and uncertainty flickered across her face. He was doing the right thing in going home so why didn't he feel better about doing the right thing?

"Whatever time is fine, then, but I should remind you that my parents will be here about noon."

She'd mentioned that they'd be over on Christmas Day.

"They'll bring Gracie lots of frilly clothes and maybe some mutual bonds or Fortune 500 stock."

At first he thought she was kidding, but at the serious look on her face he decided she wasn't. "Interesting Christmas choices for a six-year-old."

"Six. Two. Either way, it's never too young to start preparing for one's future."

Not liking the tension now etched onto her face, he nudged her shoulder. "They sound like party animals."

"Ha." She did smile, albeit weakly. "That they are not. More like some idealistic television couple. He's an investment broker. She's a country-club stay-home wife. They live in a plastic bubble of utopia."

"And you?"

"I'm not a chip off the old block. More like the daughter who should have been a son and has been a big disappointment at every point along the way."

"I doubt that. You're a very successful woman."

She gave a wry smile. "I guess that depends on what perspective you're looking from."

"From where I'm sitting, you're accomplished, beautiful, intelligent, compassionate and a good mother to Gracie." He didn't mention sexy since he didn't think that would be a trait her parents would appreciate, but he definitely appreciated that about her. "What more could they want from their child?"

Her cheeks turned pink and he could tell his praise pleased her. Guilt hit him that he hadn't complimented her more over the past few weeks, that he hadn't realized just how much she questioned herself. He should have told her over and over how amazing she was.

"They would have preferred for me to live a bit more within the rules."

Her comment seemed hard for him to fathom. "You a rule breaker, Taylor?"

"Apparently only on the big things."

His comment had been a tease, but her slight shrug made him wonder at her past. "Such as?"

"I didn't go into investments, but a doctor was a respectable profession, so they supported me in med school. Then I got pregnant with Gracie. That didn't win me any accolades in their eyes." She took a deep breath, then gave another shrug as if what she was saying didn't matter so much, even though it obviously did. "Now I've married a man I barely knew and am going to be the first in my family to divorce."

Good thing he knew she didn't want to be married any more than he did or he'd feel all kinds of guilty. As it was, he still felt a heel that their relationship caused her grief. "They don't know we're divorcing yet, do they?"

"No, and I'm grateful I don't have to deal with that on Christmas Day, but I dread their reaction when I do tell them. They've already told me how disappointed they are yet again in my life choices. If you decided not to show tomorrow, I wouldn't blame you."

"I'll be here." As uncomfortable as it might be, he would be there for her parents' visit and would hopefully be able to show her parents a glimpse of the woman he saw.

Before heading home, Slade brought in the large box containing Gracie's toy kitchen. "Is it okay if we set this up tomorrow, or would you rather put it together tonight?"

She shook her head. "Tomorrow is fine."

"Then I'll be going."

She nodded. "Tomorrow will be a long day, full of highs and lows."

"We'll focus on the highs."

"You're right. I have a lot of reasons to be thankful." Her eyes searched his, confused, tempting. "You're one of the things I'm thankful for, you know."

He stared at her a moment, wished things were different, acknowledged that they weren't and that he would also focus on the positives. He was getting the opportunity to make a difference in a deadly disease, to strive toward his goal of a cure. He didn't acknowledge her words, because what could he say that wouldn't reveal too much of the turmoil inside him?

He grabbed his coat. "I'll be back first thing in the morning."

CHAPTER TWELVE

"TELL ME THEY weren't like that growing up."

Drying the plate she held, Taylor laughed at Slade's expression. "They weren't."

"They were worse?" Slade said, helping her dry the dishes and put them away.

Taylor just smiled. Her parents had descended on them, brought presents, criticized everything from Gracie still being in her pajamas at noon to Taylor looking tired to they really should have had Christmas at their place and Taylor should be more co-operative. They'd been polite, though barely, to Slade initially. Her father had quizzed him like a drill sergeant.

Which had seemed ridiculous since they were going to divorce anyway. Only she hadn't told her parents that and neither had Slade.

Slade had laid on the charm. Halfway through their visit her father had actually seemed to accept him. Her mother's only direct comment regarding Slade had been that, after seeing him, she at least understood Taylor's temptation, even if she didn't condone her choice.

Taylor had bitten her tongue and smiled at her parents, regardless of their words. Although not touchy-feely with her, they hadn't been bad parents, just ones caught up in their own lives and expectations to where they hadn't been able to understand when their daughter acted outside those standards.

Gracie loved her grandparents. For the little girl, they had genuinely smiled as Gracie had shown them the toy kitchen, which she and Slade had put together while Taylor had made breakfast, plus all her many toys and new clothes.

Gracie had also given Slade the presents she and Taylor had picked up for him. Not once while they'd been opening presents had he mentioned a present for her. Although a little disappointed that he'd changed his mind about picking up a little something for her, she supposed it didn't really matter. More than anything she'd been curious about what he'd choose for her.

"Mr. Slade, I made you some yummy bacon and eggs." Gracie carefully offered the plastic plate of toy food.

"Looks good." Slade pretended to eat the food as Gracie beamed at him. He might not have said the words back to Gracie, but his actions were those of deep affection.

Taylor's muscles seemed to freeze as she watched them, as she tried to wrap her mind around the man playing with her daughter, the same man who'd spent the past few weeks being the perfect guy, the same man who'd gone through at least a dozen girlfriends during the past year and who had the reputation of a ladykiller. Because he was.

Or was he?

Gracie giggled as Slade pretended to sip tea.

Taylor swallowed. A vision of him walking out of her Vegas hotel bathroom wearing nothing but a towel popped into her mind. As attractive as that image was, the image of him on the floor, playing with her daughter, attracted her in so many more meaningful ways.

Who was she kidding? Everything about the man attracted her. Because she was falling for him.

Had fallen head over heels.

Just as she'd fallen for Kyle. Only her feelings for Slade were so much stronger than anything she'd ever felt for Kyle.

Her heart ached at the knowledge and moisture blurred her vision. She wanted to believe Slade was different, that he'd changed over the past few weeks.

He glanced up, caught her eye and grinned.

Maybe, just maybe, he had fallen, too. If not, she suspected she was in for some major heartache.

Slade glanced up in time to see Taylor swipe at her eyes. Was she crying? Because of her parents? They'd been uptight but hadn't been that bad surely? He'd thought by the end of their visit that they'd started warming to him. He wanted to ask if she was okay, but she scurried away as if she'd forgotten something in the oven.

He immediately glanced up when she reentered the living area. Whatever he might have seen earlier, now she was all smiles and focused her attention on Gracie.

They spent the rest of the day playing games with her, checking out her new toys. Then, with Gracie half lying on Slade, half lying on Taylor, they watched a movie she'd gotten in her stocking from Santa. Halfway through the movie she was out like a light.

"I think she had a good Christmas." Slade watched Taylor twirl a curl around her finger as she played with the little girl's hair. Prior to dozing off, Gracie had done the same, playing with Taylor's hair, which, after her parents had left, she'd loosened and worn down.

"I know she did. She was so excited over the kitchen and all the dishes and toy food. Thank you, Slade."

"I've had a great time with her today." The perfect last day with Gracie and Taylor.

"She's crazy about you." She glanced down at her conked-out daughter. "With as early as she got up this morning, she's probably out for the night."

"Do you want me to carry her to bed?"

Surprise registered on her face. "Sure. I'll go turn her covers down."

Without waking her, they tucked Gracie in, then made their way back to the living room. Taylor picked up the remote and turned off the movie. Slade, however, went to the coat closet and dug in his pocket.

"I have a little something for you."

"You do?"

He grinned. "You didn't think I'd forgotten your gift, did you?"

"You didn't need to get me anything."

"I wanted to. I just hope you like it."

"I'm pretty easygoing so you shouldn't worry about me not liking my gift," she said with a smile. "I'm not that ungrateful a person."

"I know you're not." She wasn't. She was sweet, kind, thoughtful, passionate, beautiful and his, only not really and not for much longer.

He'd put a lot of thought into her gift. Thought hopefully she truly would understand. He'd wanted to give her a gift that meant something, a gift she wouldn't toss out after he was gone from her life. A gift she'd treasure and keep forever that was from him. Why that was so important he wasn't sure, but it was.

"Here." He handed her the present.

She opened the package, saw the jeweler's box inside and hesitated. "You said it was a small gift."

"It is a small gift."

"I thought you meant cost wise," she responded, looking uncertain.

"Just open the box, Taylor."

She did and glanced up at him with tears in her eyes. "Oh, Slade. It's perfect."

Pleasure rippled through him. Mission accomplished.

"I took the photo with my phone the other night when you had her in your lap and printed it for the locket."

She pulled the necklace out of the velvet box. "Help me."

He did, clasping the gold chain around her neck and

stroking his fingertips over the smoothness of her nape because he couldn't resist the feel of her skin.

She touched the locket, which fell between her breasts. "Thank you." Then she surprised him by throwing her arms around him and hugging him.

What was Taylor doing? She knew better than to touch Slade like this. Only his gift was so sweet, so thoughtful, so perfect, she couldn't not express her gratitude.

"I take it you like it?" he asked, holding her close.

"I love it." She should move away now. Hug time was past. So why wasn't she removing her arms from around him? Why was she snuggling closer, letting the feel of him wrap around her, letting his scent envelop her, letting her body melt against his?

"I'm glad."

She nuzzled his neck lightly, knowing she should move away but needing more before she could. "What made you think to get me a locket with a photo of Gracie and me?"

"My mom used to wear one with a photo of me and her. She treasured it. I thought you might, too."

Had he just kissed her hair? He shifted. He had definitely kissed her hair. Her cheek. His lips hovered over hers, so close they almost touched, so close she could feel the warmth of his breath.

His blue eyes stared into hers, so many emotions stormed there. Emotions she recognized. Desire. Longing. Need. Confusion. She closed the tiny gap between their mouths. A guttural noise sounded deep in his throat and he kissed her back. He held her close and kissed her over and over. Sweet, seductive, hungry kisses that cast her further and further under his spell.

When he pulled away he brushed a strand of hair back away from her face. "We shouldn't do this."

Disappointment hit her. Disappointment she shouldn't

feel. She didn't want him to go. Not tonight. Not last night. Not ever. Which scared her.

She started to push him away, to tell him to leave and not come back, because truly that would be best for protecting her vulnerable heart.

Instead, said vulnerable heart pounding in her chest, she whispered, "I want this, Slade. I want you."

I want you. Had he ever heard sweeter words? More precious words? More torturous words?

He should go. He knew that. Or should at least tell her about his flight plans for the next morning before they did what they were about to do. He couldn't walk away from her. Not when he knew tonight was the last time he'd hold her, kiss her, make love to her.

He was beyond thinking about anything other than the fact that she wanted him and was giving herself to him. He couldn't walk away, couldn't do more than cherish her gift.

Hand in hand, they walked to Taylor's bedroom, pushing the door to and locking it. Slowly, in the low lamplight, they undressed each other, kissing, touching, needing, giving.

"I want you so much, Taylor." He rained kisses over her throat, her nape. It was true. With time and distance he'd get past Taylor, would move on, have other women in his life, but at the moment he couldn't imagine ever touching anyone but her. Couldn't imagine even wanting to.

"Show me," she urged, arching into his kisses.

He intended to show her just how amazing she was, and did. By the time he had pushed her back onto her bed, had prepared her body for his, Taylor whimpered.

"Please."

Please. He should be the one begging her for the privilege. Slipping on a condom, he thrust inside her, giving her everything he had to give. More. So much more because he was positive that when he left he'd be leaving behind a part of himself.

He couldn't fool himself otherwise.

Higher and higher they climbed. Heat built a sweet pinnacle that promised to topple them over the edge. So much more than anything they'd shared in Vegas. So much more than he'd dreamed possible.

Just as he reached the point he could no longer hold back the mounting pleasure, Taylor softly cried her own release and he was a goner.

Gone. Gone. Gone.

He collapsed onto the bed next to her, gasped to catch his breath, to overcome the fireworks flashing through his mind and body. Damn.

He rolled over to tell her how amazing she was, to tell her about Grandview and that he was leaving in the morning, but that maybe she could fly to Newark from time to time to see him. Or vice versa.

He wasn't opposed to a long-distance affair with her. Actually, the idea appealed a lot. There was no reason to deny themselves the phenomenal chemistry they shared.

"I don't want a divorce, Slade," Taylor told him when their gazes met. Her heart shone in her eyes and her fingers clasped the locket he'd given her. "I want our marriage to be real. For us to be real."

Oh, hell. Pain spasmed in his chest while he searched for words to say he was leaving.

If Taylor had harbored any illusions that Slade felt something for her, that he wanted the same things, the look of horror on his face quickly dispelled them. What a fool she was. What had she expected? That sex with her again would magically morph him from playboy to Prince Charming like in some fairy tale?

Just because she'd fallen for him, it didn't mean he had fallen for her. Sex was just sex to Slade. Just as it had been to Kyle. She shouldn't forget that.

"I'm sorry. I shouldn't have said that," she began, scooting away so their skin wouldn't touch. She didn't want to be touching him. Couldn't be touching him.

"Don't," he told her, grabbing her arm but not hanging on when she pulled loose. "I'm the one who is sorry, Taylor."

"You have nothing to be sorry for," she assured him, picking up her clothes off the floor and scurrying to put them back on. After all, she'd known he was a playboy, had known his reputation long before Vegas. Plus, he'd told her he didn't want to be married. For that matter, she'd told him the same thing. She'd been under no illusions except her own. Because she'd gotten caught up in their pretend relationship and wanted to believe. "This is no big deal."

"You look like it's a big deal."

Yeah, she supposed she did. Sex was a big deal to her. Always had been. She couldn't turn that off. Not the way the men in her life could.

"I've known all along that our marriage was pretend, that we were divorcing, and I had sex with you anyway. That's my problem, not yours."

"Taylor…" Her name came out as a sigh.

"It doesn't matter, Slade. I'm an adult and knew what I was doing. You played by the rules we set. This is my fault, not yours."

"I'm leaving."

She hadn't really expected him to stay the night, not after her words and his reaction, but she hadn't been prepared for his abruptness. Had she secretly hoped he'd tell her she was wrong? That he was willing to try?

Oh, God. She had.

"I know." She forced her voice to remain steady despite the pain racking her insides, making her want to curl up in the fetal position and cry at her foolish heart. "You can't stay the night. Gracie."

"That's not what I mean." He sat up in the bed, raked his fingers through his dark hair and looked so guilty she could only stare at him and wonder what he'd done. "I'm leaving as in moving."

Her knees shook and she sank onto the edge of the bed. "Moving?"

"My flight is booked for the morning."

Moving. His flight was booked. In the morning. As in he'd known he was leaving before he'd arrived this morning, before they'd spent the day together, before she'd invited him into her bedroom, before she'd told him she wanted their marriage to be real. How long had he been playing her for a fool? Was he just laughing at how easily she'd caved?

Anger hit her.

"You spent the day with me and Gracie knowing you're moving in the morning and you never said anything until *now*? Did you not think that was an important piece of information for me to have before…before what we just did?"

He had the grace to look remorseful. "Technically, I won't be moving for a few weeks, but I am flying to Newark tomorrow morning. I got the job with Grandview."

Was she missing something? "What job?"

"The one I interviewed for in Vegas."

She was definitely missing something because she'd not known he'd interviewed with Grandview. Her mind? Her heart? Her sanity? All of the above? "I'm confused."

"I told you about my mom, about how I want to make a difference, a real difference in the fight against breast cancer. I interviewed for a position with Grandview and I got the job. This is my opportunity."

She took a deep breath. "So you've known all along that moving was a possibility, but never said anything to me? Your *wife*?" She put emphasis on the last word.

"You're acting as if you're really my wife. We've just been pretending the past month, Taylor, to make things easier at work and with our families. Nothing more. We both agreed to those terms."

He was right. It had all been pretend. But she'd gotten

caught up in the pretense and had lowered her defenses. She'd fallen for him and he'd kept right on being himself. Could she even fault him for that?

"I'm sorry, Taylor. I told you from the beginning I didn't want a wife or kids. Had you been pregnant, it would have complicated our situation, but you aren't. We took precautions just then, so pregnancy shouldn't be an issue from tonight, but if so we'll deal with it."

Ugh. Hearing him talk about their making love, about a possible child they'd made, so clinically, so coldly, hurt.

"All this was to make both of our lives easier rather than face grief about marrying and filing for divorce so quickly right before the holidays, to prevent our mistake from affecting my chances with Grandview, too..."

Light finally dawned.

"That's it, isn't it?" she accused, forgetting to keep her voice down. "That's what all this was really about. Not your family or office gossip or keeping things calm until after the holidays or even sex. All this was because you didn't want Grandview finding out you'd married a woman you didn't know and planned to get divorced because you were afraid that revelation would hurt your chances with your precious dream job because they might think you flighty?"

His jaw worked back and forth. "You can't deny that this way was better all the way round, including for you."

She gritted her teeth and fought the urge to hit him. "No, you jerk, it's not better all the way round because a month ago I didn't know I loved you!"

"Taylor," he began, his expression strained. He raked his fingers through his hair again. "Please, calm down and listen to reason."

"There is no reason. You used me. The least you could have done was be honest about it so I wouldn't have bought all the looks and touches, and believed you actually cared about me and Gracie. I'm such an idiot. I knew better."

* * *

Slade pulled his jeans on and slipped his T-shirt over his head. This wasn't how he wanted the night to end. Maybe he'd known it was inevitable. Maybe that's why he hadn't told her the moment he'd found out he'd gotten the job. He'd known she'd be upset.

What he hadn't counted on had been Taylor saying she loved him. She didn't. She was just confusing unbelievably great sex with emotions.

Not that he didn't understand how she could make that mistake. He knew better, knew he was incapable of love, but he could almost convince himself he loved her, too. Almost.

The best thing he could do would be to leave. Her anger would help shield her from hurt and soon she'd realize she didn't love him. With a little time she'd acknowledge that his leaving had been the right thing.

It was the right thing.

So why did doing the right thing feel so very wrong?

CHAPTER THIRTEEN

TAYLOR MADE IT through the workday without having to answer too many questions about why Slade wasn't at work. Had Nina told their colleagues there was trouble in paradise or the truth? That Slade had left her? Either way, Taylor was grateful that the office seemed to still be on a holiday high and content to ignore her misery.

She picked Gracie up from her extended school program and focused on cooking dinner while Gracie colored a homework picture.

"I miss Mr. Slade." Gracie pouted, not looking up from where she was coloring the picture at the dining room table.

Heavyhearted, Taylor stared at her daughter. Gracie had gotten used to spending time with him every day. She'd commented repeatedly each evening that she missed Slade. No doubt this evening wouldn't be very different. Her daughter loved him. Wasn't that what she'd feared, what she'd wanted to avoid all along?

Look at what she'd allowed to happen. Not only had she failed to protect her own heart, she'd failed to protect Gracie's.

"I know, baby, but Mr. Slade is a busy man. He has important things he has to do." She'd told Gracie that Slade had gone out of town on an important trip. "He helped us a lot this Christmas, but he's not always going to be around. He has his own life, his own family."

Gracie's little face squished up. "He's married?"

That hadn't been what she'd meant. She'd been talking about his father and stepmother. Her heart thudded in her chest.

"About that…" Should she tell Gracie? What would be the point, other than that she didn't keep things from her daughter? Not usually. Why had she waited so long to tell her daughter the truth? "When I went to Vegas, Mr. Slade went with me, and we made a mistake while we were there."

Gracie stopped coloring and frowned. "What kind of mistake?"

"We accidentally got married."

"Accidentally got married?" Gracie didn't understand and Taylor fully understood that. She didn't understand any of it herself.

"I know it sounds confusing and that's because it is confusing. That's why Mr. Slade has been around so much the past few weeks. But our time with him is up."

Gracie's expression remained pinched. "Because you won't be married anymore?"

What had she done? Letting Gracie be exposed to Slade, letting her fall for his charm, letting her come to depend on him as being a part of her life? Maybe her parents were right. Maybe she was destined to always let down those she loved.

"Something like that," she admitted.

"Can't you accidentally get married again?" Gracie asked with the reasoning of a child.

Oh, Gracie! Taylor hugged her daughter to her. "Life doesn't work that way."

Gracie didn't look convinced. "Why not?"

"Mr. Slade and I didn't really want to be married."

With a wisdom beyond her young years Gracie considered all that Taylor said. "That's why it was an accident?"

"Yes."

"But why can't you want to marry him? He's really nice."

"That he is," Taylor admitted.

"Plus, he likes us." Gracie pleaded Slade's case, breaking Taylor's heart a little at how much hope she heard in her daughter's voice. "I know he likes us."

"Of course he likes us, baby," she agreed, trying to figure out how to explain her and Slade's relationship without hurting Gracie even more. "Slade especially likes you. He thinks you're wonderful."

Gracie's face took on a serious look. "Then we should keep him because I like him, too."

Taylor closed her eyes. Keep him. Sounded simple enough. Only he hadn't wanted to be kept.

"Besides, he's your Christmas present."

"What?" Taylor blinked at her daughter.

"He is your Christmas present. I know he is," Gracie insisted. "I heard you and Aunt Nina talking last Christmas when you thought I was asleep. You told her you should have asked Santa for a man." The little girl gave her a solemn stare. "At school, when we had to write letters to Santa, I asked him for a man for you, but my teacher made me write a different letter because she said she couldn't post that one on the wall."

Mortification hit Taylor at Gracie's teacher reading the letter with Gracie asking Santa for a man for her mother. Oh, my.

"So I wrote another for the wall, but Miss Gwen promised she'd send the first one to Santa. I asked him at the mall and he told me you'd gotten your present early so I knew he was talking about Mr. Slade."

"Gracie, I…" Taylor paused, not sure what to say in response.

"We should keep him," Gracie repeated. "He's a good Christmas present."

Taylor saw the longing in her daughter's eyes, knew there was a similar longing in her heart.

But she'd told him she loved him and he'd left. There was no denying that they wanted different things. Yet how did she explain that to her child? No matter what, she didn't want Gracie hurt any more than she already was. She'd known better than to let someone into her and Gracie's world, to risk someone hurting them. Lesson learned.

She pasted on a bright smile and hugged her generous-hearted daughter. "Slade was a great Christmas present, Gracie, and we got to spend Christmas with him and that was wonderful." No matter how much she ached inside, spending the holidays with Slade had been wonderful. If only doing so hadn't come at such a high price. "But now Slade gets to enjoy his Christmas present, which is to work at his dream job. As much as you and I miss him, we do want him to be happy, right?"

Taylor did. She supposed. Mostly, she just wanted Gracie not to suffer because of her mistake in forgetting who Slade really was. A playboy who wouldn't ever truly settle down.

Gracie frowned in thought. "Yes, but wasn't he happy with us?"

"He was." She believed he had been. But Kyle had been, too, at the beginning of their relationship. Men like them enjoyed life, but quickly got bored and moved on. It's just how things were. "But his new job is what he's always wanted. Because we care about him, we are happy he got what he's always wanted."

Gracie's nose curled. "I guess so."

As angry and hurt as she was by his actions, as much as she doubted she could ever forgive herself for allowing him into their lives and hurting Gracie, as much as she would never trust him again, Taylor knew so.

Grandview Pharmaceuticals was everything and more that Slade had craved for years. The clinical research director position being dangled in front of him gave him the opportunity to work directly on developing a promising new chemotherapy drug.

He'd be heading up the team.

They'd agreed to his contract terms and were having the legal documents drawn up. In the morning he'd meet with them, sign the papers and start the rest of his life.

So why was he lying in a hotel bed, staring at the ceiling and wondering if he was making the biggest mistake of his life?

Because Taylor had said she didn't want a divorce or for their marriage to be pretend? Because she'd said she was in love with him?

They never could have been anything more than pretend. He wasn't the marrying kind. He was a career man.

He thought over the past month, of the time he'd spent with Taylor and Gracie, and his insides ached.

Ached.

Because in such a short time they'd become such an integral part of his life.

Which should make him grateful the Grandview job had come through when it had. He didn't need distractions from his true destiny. He didn't need emotions blinding him to his real purpose. He'd vowed to help others, to make a difference in the fight against breast cancer, to find a cure for a disease that had taken his mother and continued to take lives.

Despite the ache inside him, that's what he needed to stay focused on. His goals. His purpose. His dreams.

Taylor wasn't a part of that.

Couldn't be a part of that.

She was better off without him.

He didn't need distractions. Just look at how thinking of her was distracting him even now.

He closed his eyes, prayed sleep would come.

In the morning he would sign his name on the proverbial dotted line and achieve a goal he'd set for himself when he'd been twelve years old.

Nothing and no one would get in the way of that.

* * *

The following evening Nina and Taylor picked up Sarah Beth to give the new big sister some playtime away from all the baby attention, and headed to Pippa's Pizza Palace. The two little girls whacked clowns, squirted lily pads and were having a great time.

Actually, Gracie had seemed much perkier when she and Nina had swung by the office to pick Taylor up. She'd had so much paperwork to wade through that she'd worked late and taken up Nina's request that she pick up Gracie and then get them dinner.

She hadn't exactly been thinking Pippa's Pizza Palace, but to see Gracie's smile, to hear her laughter, to see the sparkle in her eyes that had been missing was worth enduring greasy pizza.

Unfortunately, she couldn't stop thinking that this was where it had sort of started. Vegas was where it had truly started, but her and Slade's first real date had been here.

"You're doing it again." Nina snapped her fingers in front of Taylor's face.

She blinked. "Doing what?"

"Thinking about him to the point you totally lose touch with reality."

"Believe me, I'm in touch with reality."

"Which is?"

She stared blankly at her friend. "What do you mean?"

"What is your reality, Taylor?"

"That I lost my mind in Vegas and married a man I knew was all wrong for me. I agreed to a month of pretending our marriage was real for Lord only knows what reason. And before long, I'll be divorced from a man I never should have trusted."

Why did her words feel like daggers in her chest?

Nina frowned. "Is that what you want?"

Taylor shrugged. "It's better this way. I told him how I

felt and he left. I'm not sure why that shocked me so much. Leaving is what men I have sex with do."

Nina shook her head. "Don't compare him to Kyle. Kyle was an idiot who couldn't keep his pants zipped when there was a willing woman around. You were, an impressionable young woman who'd been kept under her parents' thumb too long. He was your teenage rebellion, not the man you are in love with, like you are with Slade."

"I was in my twenties."

"You were a late bloomer," Nina quipped without missing a beat.

"Tell me about it." Taylor sighed, knowing her friend was right. Kyle hadn't been fit to spit shine Slade's boots.

"So…" Nina prompted.

"So what?"

"You completely ignored what I said about Slade."

Taylor frowned. "I've been paying close attention to everything you've said about him."

"Yet you didn't comment on the fact I said you are in love with him."

"That's not something I didn't already know so I'm ignoring that."

"Why?"

"Because it doesn't matter. Love without trust is nothing. He left Gracie and me. Honestly, it's best that he did. Better to just get his leaving over with before Gracie and I became even more dependent on him."

"I hope you don't mean that," Nina said, so oddly that Taylor raised an eyebrow.

"Why?"

But Nina didn't answer her, just indicated toward where there was a commotion in the games section of the restaurant.

Taylor turned, but didn't initially see what had caused the commotion. Neither did she immediately recognize who was causing the commotion. When she did, she almost fell out of the booth.

Slade, followed by a posse of children, Gracie and Sarah Beth included, headed toward her.

He had lost his mind. There could be no other excuse for his current foolishness.

Well, there was one other excuse.

He'd lost his heart.

To a woman who'd fascinated him long before she'd carried on a simple conversation with him and her bubbly little girl who had, along with Nina, helped him come up with a foolproof plan to win Taylor's forgiveness.

He had to pray their plan would work.

The glare she was currently giving him wasn't an indication this was going to be easy.

Recovering from her surprise at seeing him, she murmured something to Nina about leaving and stood up.

Nina grabbed her wrist and stayed her. "At least hear him out."

"I don't want to hear anything he has to say, even if he is dressed like that."

"Sure you do, and he's gone to a lot of effort so sit down." Nina's tone brooked no argument.

Looking a bit stunned, Taylor sat back down.

A good thing because otherwise he'd feel like an even bigger idiot in the Prince Charming getup Nina and Gracie had helped him choose. They'd also ensured that Taylor would show.

He turned to the little girl who was bouncing beside him. "Princess Gracie, will you take your friends over to play so I can talk to your mom for a few minutes?"

With a really big wink at him, Gracie nodded and gathered the group of kids together, shooing them back toward the games. Several times she turned back toward them, both excitement and worry shining in her green eyes.

Maybe he shouldn't have involved Gracie.

If Taylor couldn't forgive him, would it make things more difficult that he had let the little girl in on his surprise visit? No, because he refused to fail.

"I'm going to go supervise the kids." Nina stood, paused at the end of the table and gave Taylor an encouraging look. "Remember what I said about Kyle. Don't let the past color the present."

Slade didn't fully understand her comment but supposed Taylor had lumped him into the same category as her ex. As much as he hated the thought, perhaps he deserved as much.

When they were alone, Taylor gestured to his outfit. "I take it the Grandview job didn't work out and you've hired on as a local clown?"

He glanced down at his costume. "Is that how you see me? As a clown?"

Not looking directly at him, she shrugged. "I don't want to see you at all."

"Then don't look at me, but listen to what I have to say."

"What's the point? We've already said everything we have to say to each other."

Aware that other parents in the restaurant were staring at him—and no wonder—he asked if he could sit down.

"Suit yourself, but you might have more success going in search of sleeping beauties or women with fairy god-mothers."

"I might," he agreed, wondering how he could ever have been so foolish as to leave. "But I'd rather spend the rest of my life convincing you to forgive me."

"Ha," she scoffed, still not looking at him. "You really would have more luck with a pair of glass slippers and a magic wand."

"Too bad, because there's only one woman whose Prince Charming I want to be."

She rolled her eyes. "What, did Grandview realize you hadn't brought your wife with you and you're here to convince me to play wifey again long enough to make the big-wigs happy?"

"Grandview doesn't care if I'm married or not married. Not really. Neither does what Grandview want really matter to me."

"Right, because that's so not what the past month was about."

"I don't work for Grandview, Taylor."

She met his gaze.

"I turned down their offer."

"They couldn't meet your demands?"

"They couldn't offer me the one thing in life I don't want to live without."

Her gaze narrowed. "What's that?"

"My wife."

His wife. Taylor bit the inside of her lower lip. What kind of game was he playing, showing up in a prince costume, spouting comments about not being able to live without his wife?

Her rib cage tightened around her lungs, making breathing difficult. Unable to bear to hear another word, she stood.

"I'm going outside."

She practically ran out of the restaurant, gulping in big breaths of cold air the moment she was outside the building.

"Taylor?"

No. He'd followed her. She ran to the van, opened the door.

"Please, let me finish."

She scrambled to open the driver's-side door and climbed inside. "There's no reason for you to finish. I don't want to hear anything you have to say."

She didn't. He'd left her. Left Gracie. Had broken their hearts and devastated their world.

"But I desperately want you to hear what I have to say. Please, let me tell you about this past week."

She shook her head. "No, because all I hear you saying is about you. So, you got to Newark and realized you missed Gracie and me? Is that what you're going to say? Well, too bad, because that ship has sailed."

"You don't love me anymore?"

She didn't want to admit to feeling anything for him, but she couldn't bring herself to lie. "I don't trust you anymore."

"You never did trust me."

"Sure I did. Christmas, when I wanted you to stay, it was because I trusted you, trusted what was happening between us."

"And I failed you horribly when I left?"

"Something like that."

"If I could go back, I wouldn't leave you, Taylor."

"Too bad that costume doesn't come with a magical pumpkin time machine, then, eh?"

"I never realized you had such a sharp tongue."

She leaned against the steering wheel, hid her face from him. Why wouldn't he just leave? Why was he here dressed like a prince when she knew he was a playboy?

"There are a lot of things you don't realize about me."

He walked around the van, opened the passenger's-side door and climbed in. "There are a lot of things I do realize about you. Like how much you love Gracie and how you devote your life to her. Like how loyal you are and you don't give your heart easily."

She didn't deny what he said, neither did she look up from where her forehead rested against the steering wheel. She did, however, pull the door closed to block out the chilly night air. Of course, that just closed her into her van with him.

"When you love," he continued from beside her, "that doesn't just go away because the person is a fool and lets you down."

"You did more than let me down. You let Gracie down. You left us."

"I had to go."

She lifted her head and glared at him. "Then why are you back here wearing that ridiculous costume?"

"I had to go to understand what I was leaving behind."

She swallowed the lump in her throat. "Which was?"

"My heart. I'm back because I love you, Taylor. I love you and Gracie."

His words stung her raw emotions. She closed her eyes. "You can't just pop back into our lives, say a few pretty words you think I want to hear and expect me to say everything is forgiven."

"It's what I want you to do, but it's not what I expect. Neither is it what I deserve. I know that. Which is why I'm wearing the outfit."

She shrugged. "I don't see the connection."

"I want to be your Prince Charming, but know I have to prove to you that I can be what you want, what you need, in a husband, in a father for Gracie." He reached across the console and took her hand, clasping it between his. "I want to make every day of your life living proof of happy-ever-after."

"You're crazy," she accused, but didn't pull her hand away. She should pull her hand away. Touching him had always taken away her ability to think and if ever she needed the ability to think it was now.

"I am crazy. About you. To leave you. To think I didn't need you. To not admit I loved you on Christmas night." He gently squeezed her hand. "But I am admitting that now. I need you, Taylor."

She couldn't answer him.

"You don't have to forgive me tonight or even tomorrow. You just have to give me the chance to prove to you that I am your Prince Charming."

"I don't have to do anything," she reminded him.

"Sure you do."

She arched a brow. "Or what?"

"Or else I'm driving you to my place and making love to you until you are so breathless you don't have the strength to argue with me anymore."

"That's just sex and eventually you'll tire of me."

He lifted her hand to his mouth, pressed a kiss to her fingertips. "You and I were never just sex, Taylor. Not even that first night in Vegas."

Their wedding night.

"In Newark I had a lot of time to think. I'm convinced I was half in love with you long before Vegas."

"That's crazy." Crazy seemed to be her new favorite word, but she was beginning to think it was the most appropriate word for the whole situation. Maybe they were both crazy.

He nodded. "But true. You fascinated me. I'd never met a woman who fascinated me so much, but you refused to let me get close. I'd catch myself looking for you at work, thinking about you after hours, and then in Vegas I'm not sure what happened other than I was on a high that you were kissing me back and wanted me. I think I would have done anything to have had you that night."

"You did. You married me."

"Something I'd never planned to do because I'd vowed to devote myself to fighting breast cancer."

"A noble cause."

"A lonely cause."

"Because you missed Gracie and me?"

"So much I felt like my insides had shriveled up and died. I had to come back."

"Because of me?" she asked, not really believing him.

He let go of her hand, leaving her with a sense of loss as he adjusted his fake crown. "Partially, but mostly because of me."

"But your mother… I don't understand."

He turned and faced her. "I didn't either at first. As little more than a kid, I set this goal to find a cure for breast cancer and made that my life's priority. Until you, I never let anything even get close to interfering with that."

"I never wanted Gracie and me to interfere with your goals." He'd come to resent them both for sure if they stood in his way. But more than that she wanted him to have his dreams, to fulfill them. Even when those dreams took him away from her.

"Neither did I, and you don't. You just updated them to the goals of a grown man rather than those of a heartbroken boy."

She waited for him to continue.

"As for tiring of you—" he shook his head "—I suppose that's a risk every couple takes, but I just don't foresee that happening. I love you and plan to spend the rest of my life showing you how much."

"You're planning to stay in Nashville?"

"I've already talked to Nashville Cancer Care. They welcomed me back with open arms."

"You're stepping back as if you never left."

"Have you not been listening? I left and I realized what I'd left and I want it back."

"You can't have me back."

"You're saying you don't love me, Taylor? Because I don't believe you."

"It doesn't matter if you believe me or not. I don't want you in my life anymore."

"Then you'll have to divorce me, because I plan to fight for my marriage with all my heart."

"Why?"

"Because we were never pretend, Taylor. I know you figured that out long before I did. We were always real, but I couldn't admit that. Maybe you couldn't at first either because we happened so quickly and you were scared we couldn't be real. But we were." He laced their fingers, stared at their interlocking hands. "We are real."

Tears prickling her eyes, she squeezed them shut. "How

can I believe you? How can I know this is real and that you won't leave me again?"

"You have to trust me."

"What if I can't? What if I can't let my guard down enough to trust in you, Slade?"

He took a deep breath. "Then ultimately that lack of trust will be what keeps us apart."

She nodded.

"But don't think I'll give up. Or that I won't use every resource at my disposal."

"Gracie?" she guessed.

"She is who told me I had to wear a Prince Charming costume tonight. That you had to know what she already knows."

"I can't bear my mistakes causing her pain."

"Then you have to trust me, because she loves me."

"I know she does."

"I love her, too, Taylor. More than I thought a man could love a kid. I've never known that joy before."

"If only I believed this was real."

"Believe, because this isn't a fairy tale, Taylor. It's our real-life love story."

She was crying now. A major boo-hoo fest. "I don't want to be without you."

"Then don't be." He leaned across the console, took her into his arms, hugging her close. "I love you, Taylor. Please, don't cry because of me."

She sucked back a deep breath, swiped at her eyes. "Call Grandview first thing in the morning and tell them you've changed your mind, that you'll take the position."

He shook his head. "I haven't changed my mind. My place is right here, with you and Gracie, and working at Nashville Cancer Care. It's where I want to be."

"But your dreams?"

"Are being fulfilled in a way far beyond what I could have imagined at twelve when I made my career goals. I make a difference in the lives of my patients, Taylor. Just as you do. Perhaps not on the same scale as if I helped develop a miracle chemotherapy drug, but to the patients I see each day, to the patients I hand out my sticky notes to, I make a difference."

Her heart almost burst with warmth at what he was saying, at what she was feeling. "You're right, but if research is what you want I could go with you to Newark…"

Slade's breath caught at what she'd just said, what she'd just hinted at. Not that he'd doubted that she loved him. He'd known she had. Just that he knew she was going to have a difficult time forgiving him, trusting him.

"Newark isn't what I want. I want what I thought I never wanted, what I've had the past month, only more. I want you to be my wife, Taylor. In every sense of the word. That's what I came here to show you tonight."

She met his gaze. Tears glistened in her eyes, on her cheeks. "I'm scared."

"Me, too, but what scares me most is the thought of not having you by my side every day for the rest of my life."

She nodded. "I do love you, Slade. So much."

"I know, honey. I'm so sorry it took me so long to cherish that gift the way I should have. The way I do," he corrected. "That reminds me." He paused, reached into his pocket and pulled out a jeweler's box. "I have something to ask you." He half knelt on her van floorboard. "Taylor Anderson Sain, will you do me the honor of being my wife?"

"I'm already your wife." More tears streamed down her cheeks.

"Humor me here. I'm trying to do this right this time."

She nodded, swiping at her eyes with her free hand.

"I love you, Taylor. Say you'll walk down the aisle to me, that we'll have your dad give you away to me, have Gracie as our flower girl, have my dad and stepmom there, all our friends and family to celebrate with us. Be my bride, Tay-lor. My wife. Forever."

"You really are my Prince Charming, you know," she whispered as he slipped the engagement ring on her finger.

"And you are my dream woman if only you'll say yes."

Amidst tears, she nodded. "Yes. Yes. Yes."

He leaned across the console, wrapped her in his arms and kissed her. "I'm never giving up on us, Taylor. You and Gracie are mine. You know that, right?"

She nodded. "You're mine, too. My Christmas present."

"Gracie mentioned that," he said, then grinned. "I'm thinking a Vegas honeymoon."

Happier than she'd have believed possible, she smiled at the man who really was her Prince Charming and all her Christmases wrapped up in one delectable package.

"Sounds perfect. Last time I was there I got luckier than I dreamed possible."

"I'm the lucky one."

EPILOGUE

Gracie Anderson Sain walked down the aisle toward a flower-woven wrought-iron arbor. A few dozen people sat on each side of the aisle—friends, family, some of her parents' and grandparents' coworkers.

She dropped rose petals all along the way, taking care to space them so she'd have enough until she reached her destination.

"Hi, Gracie," Sarah Beth whispered as she passed her BFF and her family. Sarah Beth's brother was sleeping, thank goodness, because, although Sarah Beth's mom had quit crying all the time, her baby brother had picked up the slack. It was almost enough to make a girl think she didn't want a baby brother of her own.

Almost.

Gracie grinned at her friend, tossed a few rose petals her way, then proceeded down the aisle in her real-life pink princess dress, complete with real tiara.

She waved at her Grandma Anderson, who'd declared her to be the most beautiful girl in the whole world, winked at her new Grandpa Sain and then took her place next to her father to wait for who she knew was really the most beautiful girl in the world.

Her mother.

Appearing at the end of the aisle, Taylor appeared on the

arms of Grandpa Anderson, who bent, kissed her cheek and whispered something that had her mom smiling up at him.

Gracie glanced up at Slade to see what he thought of his bride and grinned. Oh, yeah. That was the right look. Perfect for a Prince Charming about to marry his princess.

The rest of the ceremony went by fast and then they were kissing. Gracie had to look away even though that seemed to be all they did these days. Even in front of Grandpa and Grandma Anderson, and Gracie's new grandparents.

She liked her new grandpa, even if he did pinch her cheeks. He was lots of fun and had promised her a pony for her upcoming birthday. A pony sounded great because she liked going out with Slade on his horse. However, when she blew out her birthday-cake candles she didn't plan to wish for a pony. That would have to wait until another holiday.

Her gaze sought out Sarah Beth in the congregation. She wiggled her fingers at her friend. Sarah Beth waved back, then reached to hand her mother something out of a diaper bag.

Yeah, Gracie knew exactly what she wanted for her birthday.

Even if baby brothers did cry a lot.

* * * * *

MILLS & BOON®
Hardback – November 2015

ROMANCE

A Christmas Vow of Seduction	Maisey Yates
Brazilian's Nine Months' Notice	Susan Stephens
The Sheikh's Christmas Conquest	Sharon Kendrick
Shackled to the Sheikh	Trish Morey
Unwrapping the Castelli Secret	Caitlin Crews
A Marriage Fit for a Sinner	Maya Blake
Larenzo's Christmas Baby	Kate Hewitt
Bought for Her Innocence	Tara Pammi
His Lost-and-Found Bride	Scarlet Wilson
Housekeeper Under the Mistletoe	Cara Colter
Gift-Wrapped in Her Wedding Dress	Kandy Shepherd
The Prince's Christmas Vow	Jennifer Faye
A Touch of Christmas Magic	Scarlet Wilson
Her Christmas Baby Bump	Robin Gianna
Winter Wedding in Vegas	Janice Lynn
One Night Before Christmas	Susan Carlisle
A December to Remember	Sue MacKay
A Father This Christmas?	Louisa Heaton
A Christmas Baby Surprise	Catherine Mann
Courting the Cowboy Boss	Janice Maynard

MILLS & BOON®
Large Print – November 2015

ROMANCE

The Ruthless Greek's Return	Sharon Kendrick
Bound by the Billionaire's Baby	Cathy Williams
Married for Amari's Heir	Maisey Yates
A Taste of Sin	Maggie Cox
Sicilian's Shock Proposal	Carol Marinelli
Vows Made in Secret	Louise Fuller
The Sheikh's Wedding Contract	Andie Brock
A Bride for the Italian Boss	Susan Meier
The Millionaire's True Worth	Rebecca Winters
The Earl's Convenient Wife	Marion Lennox
Vettori's Damsel in Distress	Liz Fielding

HISTORICAL

A Rose for Major Flint	Louise Allen
The Duke's Daring Debutante	Ann Lethbridge
Lord Laughraine's Summer Promise	Elizabeth Beacon
Warrior of Ice	Michelle Willingham
A Wager for the Widow	Elisabeth Hobbes

MEDICAL

Always the Midwife	Alison Roberts
Midwife's Baby Bump	Susanne Hampton
A Kiss to Melt Her Heart	Emily Forbes
Tempted by Her Italian Surgeon	Louisa George
Daring to Date Her Ex	Annie Claydon
The One Man to Heal Her	Meredith Webber

MILLS & BOON®
Hardback – December 2015

ROMANCE

The Price of His Redemption	Carol Marinelli
Back in the Brazilian's Bed	Susan Stephens
The Innocent's Sinful Craving	Sara Craven
Brunetti's Secret Son	Maya Blake
Talos Claims His Virgin	Michelle Smart
Destined for the Desert King	Kate Walker
Ravensdale's Defiant Captive	Melanie Milburne
Caught in His Gilded World	Lucy Ellis
The Best Man & The Wedding Planner	Teresa Carpenter
Proposal at the Winter Ball	Jessica Gilmore
Bodyguard...to Bridegroom?	Nikki Logan
Christmas Kisses with Her Boss	Nina Milne
Playboy Doc's Mistletoe Kiss	Tina Beckett
Her Doctor's Christmas Proposal	Louisa George
From Christmas to Forever?	Marion Lennox
A Mummy to Make Christmas	Susanne Hampton
Miracle Under the Mistletoe	Jennifer Taylor
His Christmas Bride-to-Be	Abigail Gordon
Lone Star Holiday Proposal	Yvonne Lindsay
A Baby for the Boss	Maureen Child

MILLS & BOON®
Large Print – December 2015

ROMANCE

The Greek Demands His Heir	Lynne Graham
The Sinner's Marriage Redemption	Annie West
His Sicilian Cinderella	Carol Marinelli
Captivated by the Greek	Julia James
The Perfect Cazorla Wife	Michelle Smart
Claimed for His Duty	Tara Pammi
The Marakaios Baby	Kate Hewitt
Return of the Italian Tycoon	Jennifer Faye
His Unforgettable Fiancée	Teresa Carpenter
Hired by the Brooding Billionaire	Kandy Shepherd
A Will, a Wish...a Proposal	Jessica Gilmore

HISTORICAL

Griffin Stone: Duke of Decadence	Carole Mortimer
Rake Most Likely to Thrill	Bronwyn Scott
Under a Desert Moon	Laura Martin
The Bootlegger's Daughter	Lauri Robinson
The Captain's Frozen Dream	Georgie Lee

MEDICAL

Midwife...to Mum!	Sue MacKay
His Best Friend's Baby	Susan Carlisle
Italian Surgeon to the Stars	Melanie Milburne
Her Greek Doctor's Proposal	Robin Gianna
New York Doc to Blushing Bride	Janice Lynn
Still Married to Her Ex!	Lucy Clark

MILLS & BOON®

Why shop at millsandboon.co.uk?

Each year, thousands of romance readers find their perfect read at millsandboon.co.uk. That's because we're passionate about bringing you the very best romantic fiction. Here are some of the advantages of shopping at www.millsandboon.co.uk:

* **Get new books first**—you'll be able to buy your favourite books one month before they hit the shops

* **Get exclusive discounts**—you'll also be able to buy our specially created monthly collections, with up to 50% off the RRP

* **Find your favourite authors**—latest news, interviews and new releases for all your favourite authors and series on our website, plus ideas for what to try next

* **Join in**—once you've bought your favourite books, don't forget to register with us to rate, review and join in the discussions

Visit **www.millsandboon.co.uk**
for all this and more today!

Bullinge